The Two Most Important Days of Your Life

THE TWO

Most Important Days
of Your Life

Chad Hymas
Ty Bennett
& Don Yaeger
New York Times Best-selling Author

The Two Most Important Days of Your Life

Published by Ty Bennett

Ty Bennett
Leadership Inc.
3940 Traverse Mountain Blvd.
Lehi, UT 84043
Web: www.tybennett.com

Cover & Interior Design/Formatting by Vickie Swisher • Studio 20|20

Table of Contents

CHAPTER 1

Danny

Coach Coleman couldn't remember the young man's name.

For what felt like the hundredth time, he stared down at the obituary of his former student and his mind drew a blank even as the guests began to sit in the pews around him. He mouthed the name "Danny Morris" several times to himself, in an effort to jog his own memory of any trace of the deceased young man.

But he couldn't. In his thirty-three years of coaching basketball and teaching history at Thompson High School in St. Louis, there wasn't a student that had been that much of a mystery to him.

The reverend beckoned the funeral home soloist, a young lady in her late 20s, to approach the podium. He handed her a microphone and she began to sing "I Can Only Imagine" to the two dozen guests scattered around the small funeral home.

Coach stared at the photo of Danny's tranquil face as the soloist continued to sing. He tried to place him—most likely from a previous history class—but ultimately, he failed to conjure up a single specific memory. And, from the looks of the nearly empty funeral home, not many other people knew Danny well enough to even be there. There was much about this day that didn't make sense. Not the least of which, why Coach was there. Danny's mother had called him the night before and asked that he deliver a eulogy for a young man he couldn't remember.

Danny's body was nestled in a white casket and surrounded by colorful bouquets and wreaths. He was dressed in a fine black suit with thin, gray pinstripes. Danny's closed eyes and smooth features gave the impression that he was resting peacefully and having the most marvelous dream.

Coach couldn't help but think of his own son, Chase, while gazing at Danny. He wondered if Chase knew Danny. His son had to have been a few years ahead of Danny in high school, but there was still a chance that their paths had crossed.

I should probably call Chase when this is over, Coach thought to himself, and then the truth, Coach knew, is that Chase probably wouldn't answer. Or return his call. Coach's lip trembled and he turned his gaze away from the casket.

It amazed Coach how fast his week had changed. At the time Danny's mother had called, he had been working at home on the finishing touches to his commencement speech. He'd known for more than a month that he was going to be giving that speech, but he found himself editing it constantly. The Thompson High School graduation was exactly one week away, and his speech would also serve as his final address to the faculty and student body before he retired.

As he sat in front of his oak desk and examined his speech, he had thought back over the previous term at Thompson High— his farewell semester. The feeling was bittersweet. For Coach, his final month at Thompson had been poignant. Even though he'd executed his end-of-the-year lesson plans and teaching strategies flawlessly for the last thirty-three years, this time things were different. A surreal feeling would come over him after each day when he'd finished teaching and was left alone in the classroom with his thoughts. Coach began to see every moment as a precious opportunity for him to impart a sense of discovery and knowledge to his senior class of students before they continued on with their lives after graduation—but he could never be sure that he was doing enough, or that they were *really* listening.

In its own way, the call from Danny's mother reminded him that the students were, in fact, listening.

Nevertheless, he was looking forward to transitioning into a different phase of life after coaching and teaching as well. He wanted to travel to a variety of different historic locations and sightsee—something he'd been wanting to do all his life—and to study the game of basketball for a book he'd long desired to write. Over the years, he'd been gathering notes on the greatest coaches of all time, such as John Wooden, Phil Jackson, Gregg Popovich, Pat Summitt, and Mike Krzyzewski, among others, to discuss how they challenged their teams to win. Though it was a labor of love and would probably never land a big publishing contract, it was a personal goal that he'd always put off until later. Well, "later" had finally come and Coach was excited to finally see his project move forward.

Coach found himself restless throughout the end of spring. Since he no longer had to hold his famous two-a-day spring basketball practices anymore—one at 5 a.m. and another at 4 p.m.—to begin preparing for the upcoming fall, he initially enjoyed his long mornings sleeping in. But in the afternoons, he wanted more stimulation. He wanted to be on the court, with a whistle in his mouth, and pushing his players in drills. He'd gotten restless.

Instead, now he got in his car and drove home, where he had no idea what to do with the new block of free time in his afternoon. Like many people in their last few weeks before they retire, Coach's days were wracked with thoughts about what he'd do with himself when he no longer had any obligations.

Around Thompson High, everyone else was getting in on the celebrations and paying their respects to Coach. The student government association had organized a "Life Lessons from Coach" message board in the front lobby of the school, just outside of the auditorium; it was filled with quotes, photos, and great moments shared with Coach in his tenure at Thompson. Each day, as he walked from the parking lot to his classroom, Coach could only beam with gratitude at the love from the students. He found it inspiring and emotionally overwhelming to see the wall flooded with new postings each day. Some students, past and present, had even begun delivering bottles of antique root beer—Coach's favorite—to his classroom. That Thursday morning he'd even found tacked to the lobby board a heartfelt, handwritten note from several members of the faculty whom he'd taught when they attended Thompson High as students. They each wrote about how he'd impacted their lives and what a joy it had been to work with him.

As Coach sat before his desk and attempted to put onto paper everything he was feeling, a question weighed on his mind: How do you wrap up thirty-three years of teaching and coaching into twenty minutes? It was a challenge more imposing than explaining the political complexities of the Reformation to his students, or mentally and physically preparing his varsity basketball team for a successful season—but Coach was up to the task. It excited him to know that he'd be able to use his retirement speech as a moment to coach his students, the faculty and staff of Thompson High, in a lesson of life. He wanted his final message to everyone to be special.

Then he got the phone call.

It was nearly 8 p.m., and Coach had just taken a break from writing to prepare his dinner of lean roast beef, russet potatoes, and steamed veggies. Just as he was adding the salt that his doctor was sure to disapprove of, he heard his phone ring from the den. Coach wiped his hands and turned the oven to low. He headed through his kitchen and into his living room to check the caller ID. The number was unfamiliar.

"Hello?" he answered.

"Hi Coach," said the woman on the other end, her voice low and shaky. She was so quiet that Coach could barely hear her. "My son, Danny Morris…he was a student of yours a few years ago."

The name didn't ring a bell. "I've been blessed to have taught many students, Mrs. Morris," he replied with a smile. "How is Danny?"

There was a moment of silence on the other end of the line. "W-well," stammered Mrs. Morris, "that's exactly what I'm calling about. Danny—he admired you so much. He…" she trailed off, her voice quivering, and began to sob over the phone.

Coach's brow tightened and he felt his heartbeat quicken. He sat down on his recliner, next to the house phone, and feared the worst.

"Please, take your time Mrs. Morris," he responded softly.

"I'm so sorry," she resumed a few moments later. "I know I must be wasting your time."

"No, that's quite alright," Coach had said. He gripped the receiver of his phone and leaned forward. "Please, tell me how I can help you."

"Thank you, Coach," she gulped. "I wish I were calling you

under happier circumstances, Coach. I'm not quite sure how to put this, but Danny... my son... he's-he's... gone. He is no longer with us."

"Oh, my goodness," responded Coach, his voice low. "I'm terribly sorry to hear that, Mrs. Morris."

"Danny committed suicide a few days ago," said Mrs. Morris, almost in a hurry, as though it pained her to even speak those words. "He left a note asking if you would speak at the funeral. It's being held tomorrow...I know it's very last minute Coach, but Danny was so fond of you."

Coach fumbled for a response. He felt as though he'd been doused with ice water. He managed to eke out a "thank you" to Danny's mother, and told her that he'd be there in the morning.

"Thank you so very much, I will not forget this. You are very kind, Coach," said Mrs. Morris gratefully. "Danny talked about you all the time. He wasn't into sports, but he was a big fan of you and the team. It would have made him happy to know you still remember him."

When she hung up the phone, Coach sat in uncomfortable silence, stunned at how quickly his night had changed. A wave of discomfort coursed through him as he walked back into his kitchen. He glanced at the meal he'd prepared for himself, but no longer had an appetite. Coach went to his recliner and numbly turned on the television. He found himself staring blankly at the screen, and could only hear Mrs. Morris' pained words reverberating in his mind.

When the clock reached 9 p.m., Coach turned off the television and headed for bed. Normally he'd watch ESPN's *Sports Center* before some light reading; however, tonight was drastically different. He just wanted to close his eyes.

But sleep wouldn't come. Even though Coach felt tired from a long day of teaching and speech-writing, he tossed and turned so much that his sheets became tangled. Around midnight, he finally gave up on sleep and headed into his study to reread his commencement speech for the graduation. Initially, he'd been satisfied with it, but now, something felt incomplete. Maybe it was the fact that he hadn't eaten dinner, or that the news about Danny was now weighing heavily on his mind—Coach wasn't sure—but he now had doubts about the message he had developed.

I should focus on writing a speech out for Danny's funeral tomorrow, he thought. Coach opened up his smooth brown ledger and turned to a fresh page. He took his refillable ink pen—a replica of what Mark Twain had used (Chase had brought it back from a fieldtrip to Hannibal years ago)—to begin drafting his thoughts on a message for his former student. What ensued was edit after edit, and before long, he sighed and pushed his pen away, struggling to convey the emotions he was feeling.

Danny Morris…why can't I remember this young man? He thought with regret. He went to his closet and pulled out a stack of old yearbooks and tried to find a picture of the young man. There he was, class of 2011. But looking at the picture, Coach still couldn't place him, and he had no idea why he had the impact to lead him to be the person Danny would want speaking at his funeral.

After retrieving some root beer from his refrigerator, Coach leaned back in his desk chair and gazed out of his window. The roads were still and quiet, and the moonlight shone down on the empty streets and evergreen trees, bathing the entire neighborhood in a dark blue tint. He imagined that he was the only one awake in the entire city.

Coach sipped his root beer and thought of President Abraham Lincoln trying to write the Gettysburg Address. Had Lincoln known every fallen soldier on those battle-torn fields? Certainly not. Did British Prime Minister Winston Churchill personally know every one of his citizens that he encouraged to endure under constant bombings? Of course not. But they still managed to give meaningful, inspiring speeches. A young man had lost his life, and simply because he didn't remember Danny did not mean that he still could not be poignant and reflective. Using this realization as empowerment, Coach scribbled out a few thoughts. But even with his newfound inspiration, his mind was still clouded with the sadness that one of his students had lost his way.

By dawn, a pile of crumpled paper had collected on his desk adjacent to his miniature statues of Napoleon Bonaparte and Alexander the Great. Coach woke to find himself asleep at his desk. His clock read 6:45 a.m. He took a quick shower and had a light breakfast of toast and jam, and then made sure to call in to Thompson High to inform them that he'd need a substitute until 12 noon.

Now, hours later inside the funeral home, Coach had not been able to shake his uneasiness from the night before. He felt low on energy from not eating the night before, and he was still trying to accept the unknown circumstances of his former student's death. He clasped his hands together as family and friends continued to take their seats behind him. Coach kept his eyes forward and heard the shuffling of feet and low sniffles. He thought about the kind farewells that the students of Thompson High had left him on the message board. The notes—which now felt like a final eulogy to his career—was another reminder to Coach that, unlike Danny, he was fortunate enough to be remembered.

The reverend approached Danny's parents, who were sitting down the pew just a few short feet away. Coach had greeted them when he had arrived. Though he had many questions, he realized now wasn't the time to ask. As others came to express their sorrow, Coach slid into a spot in his pew and looked at his notes. He overheard the reverend say to Danny's parents, "We'll begin now."

With that statement, all the strength that Mrs. Morris had was long gone. Coach saw her lean against her husband, with her head bobbing slightly against his chest as she cried. Mr. Morris' face was brick-solid, yet his eyes were a cloudy red as he rubbed his wife's shoulder. Throughout the funeral home, Coach could hear weeping of Danny's family and friends over the heavy silence.

Danny was twenty-two, so he was only four years out of high school. He had thought that maybe, surrounded by the boy's friends and family, he would suddenly have a revelation of one specific moment involving Danny. But the name and the face remained a mystery and now Coach had nothing to call upon except the prepared remarks he'd struggled to write in his hand.

As the young lady finished the last line of the song, with the words "I can only imagine…" hanging the air, the reverend stepped back behind the pulpit and nodded solemnly. "In moments such as these, we must remember the lives that we touched the most," he began. "We can never fully know who is admiring us silently, so it is very important that we realize how we serve others. At the request of the Morris family, I'd like to invite Coach Coleman up to say a few words about Danny."

Coach's head jerked slightly when he heard his name called. He smoothed out his black slacks and rose to his feet. From the corner of his eyes, he could see all the heads turning in his direction. Gingerly, he made his way forward.

The house lights of the funeral home were bright, and the silence from the front of the little chapel was deafening. For a moment, Coach stared out at the gathering of Danny's friends and family without speaking. He opened his mouth to begin, but no sound came out. Coach paused and glanced towards Danny, imagining that at some stage he might have been sitting in his history classroom engrossed in the discussion. Coach had wanted to engage everyone at the funeral in a similar way, to address Danny's unfortunate departure in a way that would give instruction—just as he'd done on the basketball court or in the classroom—but he struggled to find the words.

Still facing everyone, Coach could feel his skin grow hot underneath the bright ceiling lights.

"Mark Twain once said that the two most important days of your life are the day you're born and the day you discover why," Coach said.

"Unfortunately, Danny never found that second day."

He glanced towards his former student in the casket and, for a brief moment, he saw Chase, his son, in the place of Danny. Coach clenched his eyes shut and the image disappeared. He opened his eyes, his lip quivering.

"I wish I knew how to tell each of you how to find your second day," he said, making eye contact as he spoke. "The truth is, I don't know how to teach you that. But I do know that each of us has to find meaning in our lives."

Coach continued on for a few short minutes about the importance of purpose, but he sensed the words felt empty because he couldn't connect directly to Danny. Coach did not notice that tears were streaming down his face. He managed to mumble an apology to Danny's family and friends and, wiping his face with his folded handkerchief, Coach strode back to his seat.

The reverend retook his position behind the pulpit and invited everyone to pray. Coach lowered his head, but all he could see when he closed his eyes were memories of his last conversation with Chase. *Has it really been three years since we've talked?* Coach thought. The last meeting he had with his son had not gone well. So much time had passed, but Coach could still see the anger and frustration in Chase's eyes. A wall had been steadily building between the both of them for years, and their confrontation was inevitable. Even so, he had never expected the rift that would become a seemingly uncrossable chasm between them after that argument, and now, as he sat among a family who'd lost one of their own, the disagreement he'd had with Chase seemed so trivial.

Coach squeezed his hands together and shook his head. *Why, why, why did I let so much time pass between us?* He glanced down the pew to Danny's parents, who he knew would give the world to speak with their son again; yet here he was—an invited guest— and he had not spoken a word to his own son in three years.

As the reverend finished his prayer, the funeral home soloist began another song. But Coach wasn't listening. He felt ashamed and awash with guilt. He should—no, he *needed*—to speak with his son as soon as possible. His heart pounded and his brow beaded with perspiration. Coach was suddenly aware that every passing second was another moment not spent reconciling with Chase.

As the soloist continued singing, Coach could not take his eyes off of Danny. He was not much younger than Chase, and he could only wonder what must have driven Danny to take his own life. Then, he imagined Chase having those same thoughts of loneliness, fear, and anger, and allowing those negative emotions to stew in him, month after month, year after year. Coach couldn't bear the thought of Chase feeling what Danny must have felt.

Coach anxiously sat through the remainder of the funeral service for Danny. After the reverend gave instructions for the burial at the cemetery, he closed the service. Coach, along with everyone else, slowly rose to their feet. Coach turned to the right and made his way towards Danny's parents.

Mr. and Mrs. Morris saw him approach and they both gave sad smiles when greeting him.

"The service was beautiful," said Coach. "I am very sorry for your loss. I want to thank you again for inviting me here. Today has had a profound effect on me."

Mr. Morris extended his hand. Coach took it in his own and gave a strong, firm shake.

"Coach, I want to thank you for taking the time to be here," said Mr. Morris warmly. "You've done a great service to our family. Danny would have been so happy to see you."

Coach returned Mr. Morris' smile, but inside he was torn. "Unfortunately, I will be missing the burial. Please forgive me for that, but I..." Coach paused, gazing one last time at Danny in the casket. At that moment, his mind flashed to three years ago, standing in his driveway when he'd last seen Chase. His son had tears in his eyes and his hands were balled into tight fists. Coach felt his own eyes welling up with tears.

"I will never forget this day," he said.

Coach turned and walked through the sparse funeral home and, behind other guests, filed out of the exit. It was a clear and bright Friday morning. When the cool morning breeze hit his tear-soaked face, he inhaled a deep breath. Coach strode past the hearse, and even his own vehicle. He found a nice clearing just on the edge of the woods, where the sun shone directly upon him. A wall needed to come down. He just hoped that Chase would be open to seeing him.

CHAPTER 2

Chase

On the 20-minute drive home from Danny's funeral, Coach tried four times to call Chase on his cell phone and four times, his call went to voicemail. He listened to his son's recorded voice each time, but hung up before the beep. He anxiously assumed that Chase was at work, but in all truth he was not so sure what he currently knew about his son.

At noon, Coach made his way back to Thompson High to retake his classroom for the afternoon. He took the long route to the school and, as he had done a few times every month, he drove by Canopy Oaks, Chase's apartment complex.

What followed next was familiar. Coach's SUV would bounce slightly after hitting the manhole cover, which was located after the right turn on Memorial Street. The road would climb up a small hill before a slight curve, where a few overhanging sycamore trees would brush the side of his vehicle, and Canopy Oaks—a hazelnut building with sloped, dark blue roofing—would come into view. The quick drive past the complex had become routine to Coach by then; for the past three years he had made this same pass at least once a week. He'd slow the SUV and squint hard until he saw Chase's vehicle, a four-door sedan with a small dent in the back bumper from when he hit the trashcan backing down Coach's driveway the day after getting his license. Seeing the familiar car and familiar dent, a small semblance of peace would come over Coach at the simple thought that his son was there, somewhere, in the complex.

But today his car wasn't in its usual place. Coach scanned the parking lot just in case Chase had parked in another spot, but he did not see the familiar sedan.

Honk!

Coach peered into his rearview mirror. The irate driver behind him did not seem too pleased with his five mile-per-hour creep down the road. Coach sighed and sped away from the apartments.

He picked up his phone and dialed his son's number again, this time hanging on the line. "Chase, it's your father…I know I've called a few times already, but I just wanted to leave a voicemail for you," he said. "Son, I know it's been a while since we last spoke, but please…I'd love to see you. Call me back when you get a chance."

When Coach arrived back at Thompson High, he stopped for a moment in the lobby after catching a few students posting more items on his "Lessons from Coach" message board.

Being around the students always made him smile. Heading back down the hallway to his left, Coach saw a familiar student walking much too fast and trying to avoid Coach's eye contact.

"Johnson!" he barked. "I've already seen you, son. Come back here."

Johnson—a tenth grader twice punished by Coach for skipping class—flinched. He wheeled around and squeaked, "Yes, sir?"

"Shouldn't you be in class?" said Coach.

"I'm taking my class schedule request to the front office, Coach," he said, holding up a folder. "I was late."

Coach could tell he was telling the truth this time, but he

decided to go a step further. "Fine. But what have I told you about being late? Tell me: Who were the first five U.S. Presidents?"

Johnson's eyes bulged. "I got it this time, Coach. George Washington...John Adams...Thomas Jefferson...James Madison...James Monroe...I could keep going."

Coach smiled wryly. "That'll do. Carry on, Johnson."

He turned back to the message board and saw a new photo posted in the top left hand side. The varsity basketball team had commandeered that portion of the board as their territory, but among the shoestrings, photos from two-a-day practices, and fun times on the bus, Coach saw an older photo taken from a yearbook. The photo was from ten years ago, and in it, Coach was standing on top of a ladder. He'd just cut down the nets after the Knights had won the state championship for the second year in a row. Surrounding his ladder were his varsity team from that year, all of them frenzied with emotion after such a thrilling victory. Coach could see Chase, his team captain, on the shoulders of a center who now played—well, warmed the bench—in the NBA. A huge smile stretched across Chase's youthful face. He had to have been no more than 17 at the time, but his leadership skills were exceptional. Without him, that team would have never have rallied to some key wins in that postseason.

Coach removed the photo and tucked it in his inner jacket pocket, close to his heart. Then, he checked his phone once more. There were no missed calls, voicemails, or texts from Chase. Coach sighed.

The bell suddenly rang, and his thoughts evaporated. He had a class to teach.

For the rest of that afternoon, Coach floated from one lesson to the next with his senior history class. Whenever he moved from one period to the next, he'd spend his momentary free time in sporadic attempts to get in touch with Chase. Each time his son didn't answer his phone, he felt more and more dejected.

Coach was relieved when the bell for the final period rang. He drove home with a heavy heart, his mind racing with images from Danny's funeral that morning and thoughts of reconciliation with Chase. The moment he stepped inside his front door he dropped his briefcase, shut his blinds, and crashed on his bed— undeniably exhausted from that entire trying day. Before long, the sleep that had avoided him the night before finally came.

The next morning, Coach was ready. At 7:45 a.m., after a quick shower and breakfast—and re-energized by a much-needed night's rest—he got inside his SUV and pulled out of the driveway. He had woken up with the determination that if Chase would not call him back, Coach would go see him, face-to-face. He turned out of his neighborhood and headed for the familiar route to Canopy Oaks apartment complex.

Several minutes later, Coach turned on Memorial Street, ran over the usual manhole cover, and ascended the small hill before the curve in the road. The branches of the sycamore trees smacked against his window since he was driving faster than usual, and the sloping rooftops of Canopy Oaks emerged into view.

For the first time in years, Coach turned into the complex instead of passing idly by.

Since it was early Saturday morning, so there was not much activity on the apartment grounds. A lone figure in a hoodie was doing post-jog stretches as he walked towards one of the apartment units. Coach spotted Chase's sedan in its usual spot, and pulled into an open spot near his son's car, outside the second floor of building D, apartment 384.

Coach wheeled into the spot and switched off the ignition. He placed his hands back on the wheel and stared up at Chase's door. It suddenly occurred to him that he had no idea what to do next, or how to approach Chase. How would his son react when he saw him there, unannounced? He had to have seen his phone calls and messages by now.

The figure he'd seen moments earlier was now slowly walking back up the stairs to the second floor. Coach's heart quickened as he watched the young man stop at Chase's apartment door, pause, and check his jacket pocket for a key.

Maybe one of his friends, or... something more? Coach thought nervously as the realization dawned upon him. But this time, he didn't care. He'd be happy to meet whomever Chase was affiliated with, as long as it got him his son back.

Coach opened his door and stepped out into the cool morning breeze. He walked towards building D and started slowly up the steps. The young man in the hoodie had his pockets turned out and was patting his sides, then he wheeled around and proceeded to go back down the steps, pulling the hood of his jacket down and revealing his face.

Coach's heart skipped a beat, and his foot seemed cemented to the steps. "Chase..." he said, shocked.

"Dad?" Chase responded in surprise, his blue eyes wide and brilliant in the morning light. Coach couldn't help but think that he had his mother's eyes. "I'm just going to get my spare key..." Chase stammered, his eyes darting back and forth, just like when Coach had caught him being sneaky when he was younger.

"Good morning," gushed Coach. He felt out of breath at the mere fact of being closer to his son again.

Chase's face hardened. "What are you doing here?" he said sharply.

Coach gulped and gestured lightly, searching for the right words. "I called you all day yesterday—"

"I got your phone calls, dad, every single one of them," Chase butted in, crossing his arms.

"—and I just wanted to see you. I'm tired of this distance between us. We're better than this son. *I'm* better than this." Coach finished, sighing.

Chase clenched his jaw and, for a moment, was expressionless. He nodded once and Coach saw his shoulders relax. "It's cool out, so let me go get my key. We'll talk inside over coffee," said Chase, with an edge to his voice.

Coach nodded and backed down onto the sidewalk. As Chase passed by, Coach instinctively reached out to his son and pulled him into a tight, firm hug. He felt Chase's arms tighten and then relax, and then he buried his head into Coach's shoulders and began sobbing. Coach held his son and nodded, his lip trembling, then he too began to cry.

Unspoken apologies passed between them. Coach didn't want to let Chase go. He felt as though an entire lifetime had come and gone since they'd last shared a positive moment, and the satisfaction of a simple hug made his heart swell with joy. When they pulled away, Chase wiped his face with the sleeve of his jacket. Without a word, he went to his car and retrieved the spare key from the magnetized box hidden in the wheel-well. Coach followed him up the stairs and into his unit.

When the door closed, silence enveloped the room. Chase flipped on a few lights and made his way towards his small kitchen. Coach moved towards the living room area, slowly evaluating the interior. The apartment was decorated modestly: A sofa loaded with a pile of clothes was positioned awkwardly in the middle of what Coach assumed was Chase's living room. Resting over the arm of a desk chair next to the couch was a set of freshly laundered suits wrapped in plastic. There was a box labeled "St. Louis University" full of packaged socks, warm-up jumpers, sweaters, and wind-suits next to the couch. In one corner of the room was a flat-screen TV with an XBOX One connected to it, along with a messy assortment of sports related games. It was very much the home that one would expect from a young man in his late 20s, who is straddling youth and adulthood at the same time. In a plastic container were recordable DVDs, a portable camera, and a carrying case.

Chase returned from the kitchen with two steaming mugs of coffee. He handed one to Coach, then pulled up a free chair and sat.

"Excuse the mess," he said. "I haven't been home much lately."

Coach gingerly held one of Chase's St. Louis University t-shirts and smiled. "I figured after the Billiken's NCAA tourney run you'd be busy fighting off the press."

Chase shrugged. "Dad, I'm just a video coordinator for the men's basketball team, not the president of the school."

"You're the one responsible for the Billiken's offensive and defensive preparation this past season, and a big part of their success this spring."

"I'm the man behind the curtain," Chase answered sarcastically.

"And so was Erik Spoelstra and Frank Vogel, and now they are NBA head coaches," said Coach matter-of-factly. "Keep pressing on son, there's a lot in store for you. I'm looking forward to next season."

Chase took a sip from his mug. His expression hardened again. "Let's cut the 'father of the year' act, dad. Please. I'm not going to overlook the fact that this is the first time you and I have spoken in three years."

Coach nodded. "I realize that, Chase, and not a day goes by that I don't regret—"

"Don't regret?!" Chase said with a shout, standing to his feet. "You left me when I needed you the most! How do you think mom would feel knowing you did that?"

Coach's heart quickened and his mouth was suddenly dry.

"Answer me!" Chase bellowed.

Coach's head drooped to the floor. "She would not be happy," he responded weakly. "Your mother would have been completely ashamed of *me* for our estrangement. That should have never happened, Chase, and it's all my fault." He stood as well and faced his son. "I should have been there for you, to understand and accept you for who you are—regardless. There are no excuses. I failed in my duty to you Chase, and I'm truly sorry for that."

Chase's arms now hung to his sides, as though Coach's words calmed his hot anger. He'd always been so even tempered through high school and it pained Coach to see him so explosive with a frustration that he had ultimately caused.

"Dad, when Mom died, right after I graduated college," Chase began, fighting through a wave of sadness, "I needed you more than ever. You were my best friend. Those times were hard, of course, but at least we had each other. When you disagreed with my-my... *lifestyle*, it hurt me deeply. I felt as though you hated a part of me that I couldn't control. Suddenly, I had lost *both* my parents."

Coach held up his hands, as though he were signaling a peace treaty in the most non-verbal way. "I admit…I wasn't ready. I had a lot of trouble dealing with your mother's death, and you were the only thing that I had left. In my protection and love for you, I overreacted. I'm sorry if you felt that I wasn't supportive of you.

I just didn't want you to get hurt."

Coach paused for a moment to look around the room for any evidence of any significant other. He saw nothing—not a picture, belongings, or any trace of another person.

"It's funny," he said with a laugh, hoping to break up the tension. "When I parked out front I didn't know it was you headed back to your apartment. I actually thought it was your current boyfriend, and I was so happy to know that I'd finally have a chance to get to know him."

Chase looked as though he'd been offended, but his expression relaxed. Coach couldn't imagine what it must have felt like to be on alert all the time around others—especially when concerning one's lifestyle.

"Sorry to disappoint you, dad," said Chase. "I'm single at the moment. I've been much too busy cutting video and working with the team to commit myself to a serious relationship."

Coach nodded. "When your heart is ready, your life will be, too. And I'll be there to welcome my future son-in-law when the time is right."

There was a pause, then Chase fell towards his father, his face buried in Coach's chest and his tears soaking Coach's shirt. When they both separated, a joyous laughter broke out from somewhere deep inside Coach. He had no idea where it came from, but it was infectious and Chase soon joined in on the chuckle. It was as though Coach had been holding the laugh in for three years and now, his son within arm's reach, he could finally be happy again.

Coach grasped his shoulders. "You're my son, no matter what, and I love you," he said firmly.

"Dad, I'm sorry I made this so hard on you," Chase said. "I shouldn't have ignored you."

Coach shook his head. "No. This is not your fault. It's mine. My job as your coach was to teach you and prepare you for life—not dictate every turn it was to take for you. Likewise, my job as your father is to love you and I haven't done my job well."

"Dad, you taught me everything I needed to know with Melanie," responded Chase.

Coach blinked, confused. "Who's Melanie? I thought you were interested in—you know…?"

Chase's eyes flashed. "Dad, you seriously don't remember that experience?"

Coach shook his head, and Chase beckoned him to sit again.

Picking up his coffee and still wiping his eyes, Chase cleared his throat and gazed reflectively as he recalled the details. He turned to Coach and said, "It was the fall of 2003, the season we won state, but we didn't know that then, of course. We were too focused on beating West Haven."

"They were the defending state champs that year, right?" Coach nodded in remembrance now. "I can remember that season well."

"Your 5 a.m. practices were the death of me," Chase continued.

"You were up for the challenge, as I recall it," Coach responded with a smile. "Which was why your teammates voted you captain that year."

Chase smiled happily at the thought. "You pushed us hard to get us prepared for that game. West Haven had destroyed us the past two years in a row, and no one thought that we'd have a chance against them. I admit, early on I didn't either. I wonder who's bright idea it was to schedule the best team in the state against little ol' us for the first game of the season?"

"It was David versus Goliath!" said Coach with a laugh.

Chase smiled warmly. Coach loved to see his son's face beaming.

"It was my senior year, and Mom and you were still doing spaghetti nights at our place for the team—remember those? She was feeling pretty bad but she never let on and we didn't get the cancer diagnosis until spring. Anyway, after dinner, you told us to go off and talk among ourselves to decide our game plan for West Haven. We were playing them that next week…man, were we nervous. So the guys and I went to the basement and began blasting some Linkin Park to get ourselves pumped to beat the team we'd never beaten before.

"I'm not sure when—or *why*—but at some point we started talking about this girl that went to Thompson High. Her name was Melanie, she had Down Syndrome, and one of her arms had been amputated because of a medical complication when she was a child. Well, we started to trash talk the poor girl, even though she'd never done a thing to us. We just were making dumb jokes and imitating her. Gosh, we were so dumb back then."

Coach could see that Chase was still upset with himself. As he spoke, he rubbed his hands together as if he were trying to wipe off the shame of the memory.

"I used to rationalize my actions as just a few dumb jokes that weren't really hurting anyone, but it was really bullying. These days, what we did was the equivalent to what a lot of kids face over social media. You really don't have to punch someone to be a bully. I had to learn that lesson the hard way," mumbled Chase. "Anyway, after a few minutes of us talking badly about a completely innocent girl, you burst into the room without warning, shut off the music, and dropped to one knee. I can remember all of us immediately shutting up, because you had only done that in practice when you wanted to get our attention. Everyone knew that when you'd drop a knee, you meant business."

Coach nodded in agreement. "Son, I've been doing that with my players for over three decades. It's something I learned from my former coach and mentor, as well. Coaches never teach from a higher level or beneath, but they must put themselves on the same level as their players. So the knee drop always represented an equal level of understanding from coach to player—and vice versa."

"Exactly. And one day, when I'm a head coach, I'll do the same," Chase said excitedly. "I just remember the entire countenance of the room changing when you did that. It was like—wow!" Chase snapped his fingers. "You had our attention automatically. And then you said something I'll never forget: 'I can't believe what I heard you guys say about that girl. I thought you all were better players than that. And I'm most disappointed in your captain.' And then you looked me squarely in the eye, and continued with 'But it's not your fault, or your captain's. It's mine. I'm the one that's been coaching him his entire life.'" Chase's voice got thick. "I swear, you could have heard a pin drop in that room."

The memory to Coach was grainy, but the way Chase recalled all of the details had him captivated. As his son continued, he could not help but notice that his face was flushed with a bright, moving sense of pride.

"You took the blame, even though we were the ones spewing garbage. I didn't know what to say to that, but all of our petty jokes then seemed so immature and cruel," Chase said with a sigh. "But it wasn't enough. The next day at school, as a team, we didn't do anything different. We carried on as though that discussion never happened. It was in one ear and out the other. What a waste of a teachable moment, right?

"But during lunch time the entire varsity team was sitting at our table—the cool kids on campus—and making a ruckus. We were wearing our jumpsuits, being rowdy, and thinking we were the hottest thing since sliced bread. And then you walked into the cafeteria unannounced. The entire student body clapped and cheered you on with 'Coach, Coach, Coach!' It was like an impromptu pep rally. Everyone was hyped up for the game. But you were there for a different reason. You walked straight to our table without breaking stride, and said—"

" 'Hey son, it's nice to see you. Where is she at?'" Coach said, now clearly remembering that pivotal moment.

Chase lifted a finger. "See, I knew you'd remember this! How could you not?"

"You played dumb," Coach said.

"Yup. I said, 'Who?' I was never a good actor. You told me not to play stupid with you. I was so ashamed because I thought you were there to embarrass me in front of my friends. I started to apologize to you again about Melanie and my dumb comments, hoping you'd go away. But you said, 'A coach would never want to embarrass his player. I'm here to teach you how to stand up and be a leader of a team. Now where is she?' And you said that right in front of the entire varsity squad. Everyone at the table was listening without a word—but probably as nervous as I was. I pointed to her table and you told us all to get up and follow you."

"Melanie was always happy," Coach said, now picturing the young lady in his mind as though it were yesterday. "She had the biggest smile, as though she knew some big secret that no one else was aware of."

"Most definitely. The lunchroom was so noisy, but everyone

was still watching. You led us to Melanie's table, where she was sitting alone in her electric wheelchair, smiling. You went up to her and touched the only arm she had. She shook her arm and beamed. She didn't speak clearly, so she'd shake to let others know that she was excited. It took me a few moments to realize that she was happy that someone recognized her."

"I'm sure that didn't happen very often for her," Coach replied.

"Little did she know that was about to change!" Chase responded excitedly. "You said, 'Hello, Melanie. It sure is nice to meet you. I've heard a lot about you. I know who you are.' You gestured for me to come forward. 'I want you to meet the captain of our team,' you said. I sat next to her and told her my name. Melanie was like a ball of sunshine. I just felt so guilty right then about my jokes that I was shivering. Melanie would never know, but her pure happiness in that moment just humbled me to my core. Why'd we ever think to hurt such a harmless, peaceful person?

"One by one, Melanie met the entire varsity squad. She became the most popular person in the school after that. Her lunch table was more crowded than ours had ever been! And as you talked with her, she managed to say enough to communicate that it had always been her dream to be a cheerleader. The following week, I remember the cheerleaders inviting her to join the squad, where Melanie was voted honorary head cheerleader at Thompson High that year. The *Today Show* covered it and all; I got the video clip here somewhere. The entire school came out that day for the shoot. I'll never forget Melanie shaking the Thompson pom-poms with Katie Couric herself—what a memory! The best part was when Katie asked her what the best thing about being a cheerleader was, and Melanie responded, 'Look at all of my friends!' and the crowd roared. Melanie started her signature arm shake, and we only got louder and louder because we loved to see her do that."

For the third time that day, Chase's eyes were beginning to well up with tears, but this time, they were tears of happiness. "I'll have to buy some Kleenex for the next time you visit," he said with a laugh, wiping his eyes with his sleeves. "I had no idea how profound of an impact that moment would have on my life. It motivated me to step up in my role as captain and, after we thrashed West Haven in our first game, that powered our team into a perfect season before winning the state championship that year."

Chase's joyous enthusiasm now settled into a very solemn reflection. His face and shoulders relaxed, and he stared earnestly at his father. "I have carried your lesson and example of Melanie with me ever since, from hustling for a job after college, losing mom and finding meaning, and fighting through these last three years of radio silence between you and I. Because of that moment—and many others like it—I knew that you were always a good, strong man with the best of intentions. You cared about my well-being, and though we haven't spoken in a while, on my toughest days and nights, I'd remind myself that my father taught me the value of personal character and integrity, to be a leader, and to serve others well. This always challenged me to live my life in a way that would be of a blessing to those in need. You taught me that."

Coach didn't know what to say. Chase's comments were so heartfelt and genuine that they made him think back to the previous day as he watched the Morris family bid farewell to Danny. Coach thought of how he could have served Danny—and others like him—in a better way. Reconciling with Chase had not only bridged the gap between them, but he now felt that his morning with his son was tied into a true reflection of his own life. The story of Melanie reminded him of the power in loving others and seeing the need to help them in any way possible. Dreams could be accomplished by a simple act of kindness and the best leadership truly did come from serving.

"Thank you, son, for sharing that wonderful memory with me," said Coach. He reached inside his jacket pocket and pulled out the photo he'd found yesterday of the Knights winning the 2004 state championship. "I figured that this was as appropriate a moment as any to show you this. I want you to have it."

Chase took the photo and gasped. "Simply amazing. I almost feel like I'm still there. That moment was so amazing…and Melanie started it all." He lifted his head and pointed to a figure standing in the photo. "Have you kept up with Sparks lately?"

"You two were inseparable! He was like my second son," Coach answered, "But no. I haven't kept up with Sparks since he joined the military after two great seasons at Kentucky. Is he still enlisted?"

Chase shook his head no and a glint of sadness flashed in his eyes. "He's downtown, in Mercer hospital. He got back a month ago. You need to go see him. He's in a rough spot—his girlfriend just left him and—well, I know it would do him some good to see you again."

Renewed vigor filled Coach's bones. "You can count on it Chase."

CHAPTER 3

Sparks

Coach spent the better part of his Saturday with Chase reliving old memories, watching DVDs of game film, and talking basketball. Their rapport was so natural, it was as though those three years of silence had never even passed between them.

Coach shared with Chase his previous day with the Morris family, and his regret in not being able to help Danny before he made his fateful decision.

"Dad, you have to take those leftover emotions and to do something special with them," Chase urged. "This is your opportunity to serve others, those you can still touch and help, just like you did with Melanie and in coming here to visit me. And that's all the more reason for why you should visit Sparks."

After lunch with Chase and making plans for dinner the following week, Coach said goodbye to his son and, after a quick stop by the school where the weekend janitor let him in, he made his way to Interstate 64 East, filing in with the rest of the traffic. Ten minutes later, he'd reached midtown St. Louis. Coach exited onto Grand Boulevard and made a right.

Midtown St. Louis, or the "second downtown" as it was nicknamed, was a remarkable section of the city that was as historically diverse as it was eclectic. Colorful, art deco style businesses stood sidelong with commercial buildings, and the neighborhoods consisted of classic townhomes. Many of the surviving historic building and structures had been adapted for new uses. After a few minutes of driving, Coach's GPS led him to 915 North Grand Boulevard. The square, grayish structure of the Powell Symphony Hall came into view first, but across the street from that was Coach's destination: the John Cochran Division of the Veteran Affairs Medical Center.

Coach pulled up to the visitor's parking lot, took a sticker, and found a spot not too far from the entrance. The VA building loomed before him, an eight-story structure made of light-colored brick and marble. Coach exited his vehicle and headed for the main entrance, with a gift-bag for Sparks in tow. To his right, an American flag whipped in the afternoon breeze.

Once, inside, he approached the front desk and smiled at the receptionist.

"Hello there," said Coach, warmly. "I'm here to see Sparks."

The receptionist stared at him for a moment with a raised eyebrow. "Do you mean...Jonathan Sparks?"

Coach put his hand to his forehead, as though to clear up his thoughts. "Yes! I apologize. I used to coach him in high school and that was his nickname. Forgive me for the confusion."

"No worries, he's one of our most popular patients. And he still goes by that nickname," she replied with a laugh. She told him that Sparks would be in the burn unit, but she quickly corrected herself when she looked up his information in the computer. "Actually, he's going to be moved to physical therapy soon, but you should have time for a bit of a visit before he has to go."

After receiving directions to his room, Coach headed for the elevator, thinking about the ever-smiling face of Sparks. He had watched him blossom from a gangly freshman who was all knees and elbows to a highly sought-after recruit who became an incredible point guard for Kentucky. Sparks had come from a military family though and had always been patriotic, so Coach was not surprised when he left school after his sophomore year to enlist in the Marines.

Once the elevator reached Sparks' floor, Coach bypassed a pair of physicians and a patient on crutches in his walk down the hallway. He spotted the physical therapy rooms, full of equipment; several trainers and their patients—many of whom were missing arms, legs, or were in wheelchairs—were working hard inside. Coach could hear a couple of expletives during painful stretches or a particularly difficult maneuver, and he couldn't help but smile at their determination.

When he reached Spark's room in the burn unit, Coach took a breath to ready himself before knocking softly on the hardwood door.

"Come on in," he heard a familiar voice call out from within the room.

The first things Coach saw as he stepped inside were a couple of large backpacks with the Wounded Warrior emblem plastered on the sides and back. There, sitting on the hospital bed, was Sparks. Coach could only see his outline due to the tightly drawn shades that shut out almost all of the light. He steeled himself for the worst.

He'd remembered Sparks as an energetic teenager with ebony skin, and hair curlier than sheep's wool, but the figure who switched on a dim lamp was barely recognizable as the same person. Sparks had lost some weight and gained some height, but that was hardly the surprising thing: His once vibrant brown skin was now covered in large, pink splashes of recovering burns. Sparks' hair was cut very low, but a large section of his head was completely free of any hair—only scar tissue. His arms and legs were also overwhelmingly pink, with only spots of his original skin visible. Coach could only imagine that the burns continued under his gown, and he felt an overwhelming pang of sadness.

Sparks squinted at him before breaking into the familiar wide grin. "Coach!"

"I've missed that smile and your laugh Sparks," said Coach. "Back when you played for the Knights, you used to always have that goofy expression on your face, right before I made you guys run."

"Coach, you know me, man—I think *everything* is funny," exclaimed Sparks, leaning forward with a wince. He shook Coach's hand tenderly.

"Then you'll love this," Coach said, reaching into the gym bag he'd brought. He removed a pair of worn basketball shoes from the bag. "Do these look familiar?"

Sparks began to laugh and shake his head. "My lucky sneakers! No, you didn't Coach! Really?! Where'd you find these old puppies?"

"You left them back in the practice gym, right before your graduation!" Coach said. "I always kept them in the locker room, just in case you decided to swing back by to pick them up. I just retrieved them half an hour ago. Now they are back in good hands."

"Thanks for that. I scored twenty-five on West Haven in these bad-boys," he commented, holding the shoes.

Coach took a seat next to Sparks and placed his hand on his. "How are you holding up, Sparks?"

Sparks stared at him reflectively. "Well, I decided that I wanted to be more beautiful, so I'm getting the Hollywood full-body transplant done," he joked, gesturing to his pinkish skin. "You came a month too early, Coach! We're only halfway finished!"

They both shared a laugh, and Sparks then grew more serious. "All of this happened in Afghanistan, early last year. My squad and I were performing a routine refueling when, out of nowhere, we came under fire from the hills. Corporal Rowland's gun jammed so I pushed him down and turned back around to fire at the enemy. The fuel hose had come loose and was spraying gasoline all over the place I got a face full of it. But there was too much going on for me to care about that, at the time. The bullets were landing all around us, zipping and scorching the air. I don't know how I made it back behind the truck, but I did. The firing stopped, and I saw that Rowland was okay and just for a moment, it was peaceful. Then there was a spark from somewhere—ironic, right Coach?—and my entire world went up in flames.

"I blacked out, thank goodness, so I don't remember what happened next, but I was told that my squad was able to extinguish the flames and later took out the enemy." he exclaimed, with pride in his face. "When I came to, I had been flown to Germany where I was initially treated for the severe burns on my head, neck, arms and midsection. I was sent to the U.S. where I spent time as an inpatient in San Antonio after receiving skin grafts for the majority of my burns. After that, I was sent here—home. I've been in physical therapy for the past month."

"How has that gone for you?" asked Coach.

"Pretty good, actually," answered Sparks. "I've lost a lot of strength and my endurance was incredibly low when I started, but I stuck it out, Coach. Just like I stuck it out with the skin grafts. I just chalk it all up to how I handle the therapy. Since I've played sports my entire life, I could relate to the process. As a freshman playing for Thompson, I had to learn how to improve my weaknesses. As a starter at Kentucky, I needed to learn quickly how to play with some of the best basketball players in the country. Now, as I recover, I know that each day is a battle. The Marines taught me to go above and beyond, and that doesn't have to stop simply because I got wounded."

As Sparks talked, Coach could not believe how full of life and enthusiasm he seemed. He'd come into the room expecting to see his former player in a dark depression, but it was quite the opposite. Sparks was still Sparks, no matter what had happened to him.

"I admit, it wasn't easy at first," Sparks said, almost as if he were reading Coach's thoughts. "I didn't know how to handle my scarring, because I was now pink in places that I'd always been black before. It was very hard to accept that over half of my body had been burned, and much of the damage would be irreparable. Coach," he said quietly, "after the skin grafts, I couldn't even recognize myself in the mirror. I didn't want anyone to see me. A few months ago, I'd have refused any visitors."

Coach couldn't imagine the amount of emotional pain and mental anguish that the accident must have had on Sparks. But here he was, talking with pride and hope. "Sparks, with all due respect, that's not the person that I see right now. You look so empowered."

"I am," he said with a grin. "And it's all because of the incredible support I had after I returned to the States. Man, I was in the dumps then. I had a couple of guys who were former Marines and Army who were also burn patients come to the hospital and talk with me. I'd have never recovered emotionally the way I had without them encouraging me to get out there and live my new reality—and showing me that it really could be done. I had been surrounded by doctors and nurses and hospital equipment for so long, I was almost surprised that the outside world still existed the way it did, and that it felt so…normal."

Coach listened with great interest as Sparks told him how one Marine named Nathan King had visited Sparks to deliver one of the WWP's specialized care backpacks invite him to a Spurs game. "I credit King and all those guys with reinvigorating my passion for living. They taught me that my life doesn't have to stop just because I got injured. I was always going to be me, no matter what I looked like."

"Well, the fire was a defining moment in your life," exclaimed Coach.

Sparks squinted a bit before answering slowly. "You know what? I don't think that was a defining moment."

"What do you mean?" Coach said.

"For me, that happened and I had no control over it."

Spark's comment was so short and simple, but so very profound to Coach. "And you'd like to control what defines you," he said, his voice low.

"Exactly, Coach," said Sparks. "I'd have to say that my defining moment was actually three months later, when I was lying in the hospital and King walked in. I was at a fork in the road with my life. I could keep going on, ashamed of myself and my predicament, or I could keep on living. I chose to live, and soon afterwards, things began happening. I was invited out to participate in a track and field event with other injured veterans, and I started to volunteer more with meeting and talking with soldiers and Marines who were just starting their recovery. And now, I've realized that I'd like to work with the Wounded Warriors full time when I recover.

Like King and all those other men and women I met, I want to share the renewed happiness that I have in my heart with those that need it the most."

Coach began to think about the last few days of his life, from getting the phone call from Danny's mother, the funeral, reconnecting with Chase after all that lost time, and now seeing what had happened to Sparks. In truth, he'd questioned why so many events had happened that seemed so tragically devoid of meaning, but it was there, sitting with his former player, that he realized he'd have to use those experiences to create his own defining moment in life. Like Sparks, it didn't have to necessarily be an event, but a realization.

"I'm so proud of you. I can't wait to hear what's next for you, son," said Coach, fighting back the tears.

Sparks grinned. "Neither can I, Coach."

CHAPTER 4

Shannon

Coach and Sparks talked for another hour—about Coach losing his wife to cancer, about Chase, about all the unexpected turns life can take—when there was a sharp knock at the door.

"Sparks, it's time for your afternoon therapy. It's arms and shoulder time, baby!" exclaimed a happy voice.

"You know those are my favorite, Shannon!" Sparks laughed, cupping his hands over his mouth to call back toward the opening door. Coach turned to the right to see a nurse enter the room.

"Another visitor, Sparks? You're going to have to get a secretary!" she said, looking towards Coach.

Coach stood to shake her hand, and also to move out of the way. She appeared to be in her mid-forties, and moved with both elegance and enthusiasm. Her face seemed like that of someone he'd known before but, like Danny, Coach couldn't place her in his memory.

"Hello there," he said, "I'm—"

"Coach Coleman!" cried the nurse, hugging him. "I'm Shannon Mitchell, the RN. And I'm also a former student of yours!"

Coach wagged a finger. "Well, there you have it. Last time I heard about you, your paper on Florence Nightingale was published in the *St. Louis-Post Dispatch* for an essay contest or something, is that right?"

"I can't believe you remember that!" Shannon exclaimed.

"Coach, I've been meaning to speak with you for a while. Let me make sure Mr. Sparks here makes his therapy appointment, but can I meet with you in the cafeteria—say, in half an hour? Good. I'll see you then," she said, helping Sparks get into his shoes.

Coach was caught off-guard. At Thompson High, he was notorious for keeping a solid schedule with students, teachers, and staff, but Shannon the nurse had simply worked her way into his day as though it were second nature. Impressed, he replied, "Sure thing, Shannon."

Coach bid farewell to Sparks as he was heading out of the room and promised to visit him again in the next few weeks. He gently closed the door behind him and followed the signs to the hospital cafeteria. On his way, he spotted several plaques displaying the employees of the month. He was astonished to notice that Shannon appeared more frequently than any other nurse or member of the staff. Her infectious energy back in Sparks' room reminded him of the locker room pump-up speech that Chase would give the team shortly before they went out and played their games. He was interested in seeing just how Shannon operated within the hospital.

Instead of making a left and heading to the cafeteria, Coach turned around and went back towards the physical therapy rooms. Leaning around the corner he saw another round of veterans working out at their various stations and in the rear of the room. Coach could pick out Sparks curling resistance bands away from body with his elbow resting on his waist, while a male physical therapist watched attentively at his side. He was sweating and panting, but showed no intention of quitting. Coach leaned in a bit further and saw that directly behind him, Shannon was counting his reps and shouting words of motivation.

"Keep it going, Sparks, push it!" she said. But before long, she'd moved over to the open floor mats, where another veteran was stretching out her body. A look of pain crossed the young woman's face, but when Shannon appeared to encourage her, even help her maintain her body posture, the woman continued with the stretching routine. Coach watched in awe as Shannon moved from station to station, encouraging, motivating, and supporting each of the veterans. She was like a non-stop bundle of energy, and probably the best floor general Coach had ever seen. Her eyes blazed at every turn, and she moved swiftly with decisive words and an indomitable spirit.

Coach left the physical therapy room in amazement. When he finally reached the cafeteria, he sat at a table near the door, enjoying a lemon water and some crackers, when Shannon bounded into the room. She waved and headed in his direction, but called over to the cafeteria workers as she walked. "Fantastic work today, team!" she cheered, flashing them a thumbs-up. The workers' faces immediately brightened, and they waved back.

Coach stood to welcome her, and then retook his seat. "You're like a celebrity around here," he said in wonder.

Shannon grinned. She had tied her hair back into a ponytail and had changed from her gym wear and into green scrubs. "Everyone is a superstar here. I just make sure that no one ever forgets it!"

"I have something to confess," Coach said, lifting up a hand. "I did not come directly to the cafeteria. Instead, I watched you for a few minutes while in physical therapy. I had no idea you were one of the therapists as well."

"I'm not," Shannon admitted with a smile. "It's just something that I love to do. It gives me energy. Working here, you meet two types of people: those who are very inspiring, and others who are in dire need of inspiration. I was born to inspire others during their healing processes. And it's all because of you, Coach."

Coach's eyes bulged and he almost spilled his water. "Me? Shannon—you're incredible. What I saw in there has shown me a motivation that I've rarely seen in life. I think you should take more credit for that."

She closed her eyes for a moment and nodded. "That's very kind of you, Coach, but without your influence, I'd have never gone down the road to nursing. Like I said, I've been meaning to catch up with you for quite some time. So when I saw you in Sparks' room, I was overjoyed."

Shannon then went on to say that back in 1986, when she was a freshman at Thompson High, she desired to be a trainer on the basketball team. Her father had played basketball in college and had raised her on stories of the hardwood. "We used to play with his first aid kit after a game of H-O-R-S-E and he'd show me how to add tape, lace up sneakers, and proper stretching routines," Shannon said, reflectively. She knew at a young age that she loved the sport, but by high school what she really discovered was that she loved the idea of motivation and using first aid to assist others.

"This did not become evident to me until I took your tenth grade history class," she revealed. "You introduced my class to Florence Nightingale as we studied the history of the Crimean War. I can still remember your words: 'The great peacemakers and healers of society often go quietly in the pages of history… but not in my class!'"

Shannon was laughing now, and Coach could feel himself laughing, too, from her radiant enthusiasm.

"My mother was an English teacher, so she raised me on the classics. I think back to how I went home after your class and asked her about this Florence Nightingale person…and lo and behold, Mom had a diverse collection of her essays tucked away in our small, in-house library. That weekend, I devoured everything I could find on Florence. I was absolutely obsessed with her strength, compassion, and eloquence!"

Coach's heart swelled with pride. Shannon was exactly why he'd become a teacher. She'd taken a moment from his class to heart, and had used it to chart her path in life. He couldn't wait to hear how she'd gotten into Veteran Affairs.

"Learning and writing about Florence Nightingale that semester inspired me so much to make a difference in my life," she added. "That next year, I began candy-striping at a few local hospitals. That continued throughout my junior and senior year in high school."

"And your paper on Florence was absolutely remarkable," said Coach. "I still use it as an example to my students when I teach that assignment."

Shannon blushed. "It was all because of Thompson High and teachers like you, who not only helped me dream bigger, but to find a large purpose in life. I never expected the *St. Louis-Post Dispatch* to publish my paper after that contest. When I wrote that paper, I just knew that if she could be a hero to so many, then I wanted to be a hero to at least a few. Her incredible service and your teaching are what led me to becoming a nurse."

"History is alive, that's what I always try to get across to my students," Coach said. "Whenever I taught about Florence, I wanted everyone to identify with a person in history that they could also admire. You did that, and also used her as a future model for success."

"Consider it a job well done, Coach," she grinned. "After college and becoming a registered nurse, I worked in a few hospitals; but it wasn't until I found myself at the VA that I realized that I was living my dream," she said, gesturing around her. "I've found that being able to help these veterans—people who have sacrificed so much—is what makes me alive," she said.

Coach thought back to his previous hour with Sparks, and how he'd said that his defining moment was when he decided to live his life despite his burns. Coach could now see that Shannon's path was similar.

"Shannon, I'm so happy to see that you're adding to that legacy, and that I provided help to you when you were a student. That simply is a joy to me!" exclaimed Coach.

She showed him photos of her husband and two daughters, and Coach told her about his plans for retirement once he left teaching behind. "Like you're ever going to stop teaching!" she laughed.

"Oh, no!" Coach protested. "I've put in my papers to the school system and everything."

"That's not what I meant," she smiled. "You don't need to be in a classroom to teach. You're the sort of person who is going to find a way to keep inspiring everyone—even if it's the gift shop clerk at Mount Vernon or the tour guide at the Alamo. You just have a special talent for making people learn things about more than just history."

When they both bade their goodbyes, Coach strode slowly back to his vehicle. Night was falling by now and he stared into the stars, thinking about Chase and Sparks and Shannon...and Danny. And how he had touched each one of their lives—and how they were now causing him to examine his own.

CHAPTER 5

Christopher

Coach drove home with the radio off and windows down. He marveled at how phenomenal his entire Saturday had been. That morning, when he had climbed out of bed, his only hope was that he'd be able to revive his relationship with his son. And now, at nearly 8 p.m., he'd not only done just that but had also reconnected with two former students—and he'd picked up some valuable lessons in the process.

When he arrived back home, Coach was famished. But before he began to prepare dinner, Coach took a moment to play all of the missed messages that had been stored on his home phone voicemail. The messages went back several days, which did not surprise him. End-of-the-semester grading, preparing for the commencement speech, Danny's unexpected funeral, and Coach's whirlwind Saturday had taken all of his attention.

"...*message #5, Thursday, 11:45 a.m.*" crooned his voicemail. Coach was in the kitchen and cutting open the frozen fish when a scratchy, weary sounding voice blared through his phone speaker.

"Hey, uh...Coach Coleman, how are you, pal?" the voice slurred. There was a hacking cough away from the phone receiver. "Excuse me. Coach, it's Christopher Harris—remember me? I'd love to meet up with you when your time allows. I'd like your advice on a change of career. Call me back when you can, and let's get together..."

The message ended, and Coach paused over his cutting board. Unlike Danny and Shannon, he knew right off exactly who Christopher was—from his incredible rise to his dramatic, public fall—and so did everyone in St. Louis. He'd been the crown jewel of Thompson High for his four years there—the last of which was Coach's first as a brand new teacher—and Christopher, now in his early fifties, was a successful businessman and vice-president of the controversial Acres Financial Group, still loved basketball and the Thompson Knights. As an alumnus, he'd generously donated thousands of dollars to the school over the years, along with annual, personalized notes written directly to Coach about how impressed he was at his leadership ability. However, Christopher's letters had not come in quite some time and his donations been dwindling until they simply dried up in the past year with no explanation. Coach knew well that no one was obligated to send money to the school, but Christopher had built a reputation of being a generous contributor and Coach worried had had fallen on hard times. When he'd last heard of the generous Thompson benefactor and basketball fan, it was on CNN a few months ago, when it had been announced that the CEO of Acres Financial Group was being indicted for embezzling millions from the company. And now, here was his former business partner Christopher, on Coach's voicemail—and drunk dialing, of all things.

Coach glanced at his calendar and at all of the strikethroughs for the previous month. A list of potential calendar appointments were tacked to his thumbnail board next to his key rack. The warm feeling he had been enjoying reflecting on his day was rapidly fading. He moved to his phone to delete Christopher's voicemail, when he thought back to how Shannon had worked her way into his schedule, and how blessed he'd been by her interaction.

Coach's finger paused above the "delete" button, then moved over to "repeat." He replayed the message and listened closely to the underlying tone of Christopher's voice. There was something in his phone call that sounded desperate, as though he needed a friend and an honest opinion. Coach couldn't quite say what it was, but when he stared at Sunday's only appointment on his calendar—his weekly lunch at his favorite diner, Vic's— something told him to return Christopher a call and with an invitation to join him the next day.

He reached for the phone and dialed Christopher's number. The man answered abruptly, as though he were waiting by the phone. Coach introduced himself and apologized for the delay in returning the phone call. "It's been quite a week, Christopher," he said. "But I'd like to see what your plans are for tomorrow, around noon? I'll be dining at Vic's and I'd like for you to join me."

"Coach Coleman, I wouldn't miss it for the world. Thank you for returning my call, sir," he said with gratitude.

That next day, Coach Coleman was waiting at Vic's a few minutes before his appointment with Christopher. He took a bite out of his bagel and shuffled away the sports page of the *St. Louis-Post Dispatch*.

"Coach! I didn't hear you come in. How are you this week, ol' pal?" shouted Barney, owner and manager of the diner, from behind the bar.

"I'm doing pretty good," answered Coach with a nod. "Say,

have you ever had a moment in your life where you just wonder…
what does it all mean?"

"Coach, I ask that question every time I get the bills for next
month," Barney shrugged as he stacked mugs into the freezer.
"Here, here," saluted Charlie, another regular, who raised his glass
of iced tea in a toast.

"Charlie, slow down man, it's not even noon yet!" Coach joked.

"I'm just working ahead of myself," Charlie answered.

It was another typical Sunday at the diner Coach had found
twenty years ago. Back then, Vic's was ran by Barney's father, Vic
Mahone, who'd hit it big with some of the best names in blues and
jazz during the 1960s and 1970s. After that, he'd settled down
in St. Louis and created one of the city's most famous diners—
which doubled as a bar and nightclub when the sun went down.
On the walls of the large, pill-shaped interior of the diner were
photos of Vic with B.B. King, Louis Armstrong, Miles Davis, and
Eric Clapton, all of whom had dined at Vic's at one point in time.
Coach always felt welcomed there, and for the past decade he'd
made it a weekly occurrence to eat here, where one could find a
good friend after only a brief introduction.

As Barney refilled Charlie's glass, the front doors opened and
in stepped a man dressed in a three-piece suit and shiny, buffed
shoes. He looked as though he belonged in a penthouse suite at
The Four Seasons or in a country club instead of at Vic's. A couple
of the other customers' heads swiveled to see who this posh new
guest was. At the bar, Barney squinted as though he was trying
to place where he recognized the newcomer from. "Christopher,"
Coach said, waving a hand.

Christopher shuffled over to Coach's booth and sat down
heavily. When they shook hands, Christopher held on for just a

second or two longer than Coach would have expected.

"Thanks again for seeing me, I really appreciate this," remarked Christopher, flashing a strong grin. He took a moment to press down his already slick hair.

Dolores the waitress appeared seemingly out of nowhere. She had a large pot of coffee in her hands. "Decaf or regular, gentleman?" she said.

"Oh, none for me Dolores. I'll just have my regular," Coach said.

"Uh," stammered Christopher. "I'll have two coffees, both black, each with four sugars."

"And I thought I was pushing it…" Coach heard Charlie say from the bar.

Coach smiled and clasped his hands together. "Christopher, it's great to see you again. I feel as though we've talked far more recently due to our yearly letters but I guess it's been over 30 years since we sat down face-to-face."

Christopher smiled. "Same here, Coach. I apologize for not writing you this year, but, well…as you probably know, I haven't been doing so well."

"I can only imagine how you've been holding up Christopher," said Coach somberly. "I've seen the story on the news lately, but I'd rather hear everything from you."

"Of course. I'd like to do that as well rather than allow the sensationalist news media rip me to shreds," Christopher replied with a shrug.

Dolores returned with the coffee, and Christopher paused to take a sip and gazed around the room. "I love this little place Coach. I grew up poor and my dad used to like to take me to diners and dive bars like this, simply because the food was cheap and he didn't know how to cook. Later we graduated to TV dinners, but I still preferred the dive bars," Christopher said with a wink.

Coach thought back to his voicemail, where his words were slurred and he was obviously inebriated.

"Growing up without much was motivation for me to be successful. I always wanted to be a part of something bigger than the poverty I had as a child. My first experience with leadership was as student body president of Thompson High, back in the day," Christopher explained. "It was inspiring and I desired to do more in the community, and for the people of this city. I was such an idealist back then, but that passion took me to great places and I met some great people during internships in college. Before I knew it, ten years passed and I was a founding partner of Acres Financial Group. Just like that—boom! I'm making over a million a year."

"Through the 1980s, you were on the cover of every fortune and business magazine," said Coach.

Christopher nodded nostalgically. "Those were the good times. Mark, the CEO, didn't like the spotlight very much. So as Vice President, I made sure that I was the face of our company. I admit, early on I was a fast-living jetsetter who spent money as though it grew on trees. After I matured and had a family of my own, I knew that I had to give back to society in a way that wasn't selfish. In the late 90s, I wanted to change the way the United States did finance. I worked hard to create new initiatives so that people like me—who were also growing up in poverty—would have a shot at a good life. This was one of the major reasons I became a donor to Thompson High. I wanted to add to the great school that had shown me my path in life.

"On a national scale, I was also ready to change finance in America with some key initiatives that would help people who were really struggling—I'm talking deferred payments for student loans, credit vouchers for public service, and subsidized payments for those under the poverty line. Even though we were best friends, Mark and I would get into spats about this. He thought it wasn't financially sound to invest in helping people, but I fought back, insisting that this was the future of America in our hands. It was a constant tug of war."

"A power struggle ensued?" Coach asked.

"Exactly, but not in the way you'd imagine," Christopher admitted, taking another sip of his coffee. "Mark wanted us to keep all of our resources in mortgages, since in the 1990s and early 2000s, we'd made a fortune off of it. I'd secured government funding for our new initiatives that would help out millions of people, but our bread and butter was mortgages. So we followed Mark—and then the housing market collapsed during the recession."

Coach sighed. "Everyone has horror stories from the recession. I can remember taking in a few of my players when their parents had to go out of state for work. But Acres Financial Group survived, right?"

"We did, but we took a major blow over those next few years as we recovered. Once the market stabilized around 2011, I saw the opportunity to introduce my new initiatives to my company. Without a card to play, Mark finally ran with the idea—and it was a hit! I'd have never expected that a financially humanitarian-centric cause would bring us so much new business. Our company was back from the dead!"

As Christopher spoke, Coach could see his eyes glowing with

happiness. He could tell that this was something very near to his heart. It pained him to know what was coming next.

"All was going well, and then a few months ago, this happens," Christopher said, holding up a folded newspaper that read: *Acres Financial Group CEO Embezzles $12 Million from Company.*

Coach didn't say a word, and allowed Christopher to have his moment. He sighed and stared out into the street. "It still bothers me so much, I can hardly sleep. Mark had stolen all of the funds from my initiatives, along with other company funds, right from under our noses. Even though he's in jail now, the company was shattered beyond recover and was shut down. Now, our three thousand employees are all unemployed."

"Christopher, I'm so sorry to hear all of this," Coach said with a heavy heart.

"Well," he said, "that's kind of why I wanted to see you. You see Coach, I've always admired you and the way you've coached those young men at Thompson. Five state championships and also one of Missouri's most celebrated teachers—you are truly one of a kind. I keep up with everything you do, and I have always felt guys like us were cut from the same cloth. We grew up tough, made something out of nothing, and desire to give back to society. I guess what I wanted from you was a friend. I'm going through a tough time right now and with the company failing, many of the fake people in my circle have filtered themselves out. I'm just trying to figure out what to do next, and I need an honest opinion."

"Many people re-launch their lives, just like you Christopher," said Coach. "You mentioned the recession. I can't tell you just how many former students and professionals came to me for advice during those bleak years. It compelled me to develop a portion of my history class on mastering change."

"Mastering change?" repeated Christopher.

Coach nodded. "Yes. It's about controlling the next step in your life. Many people in history have failed to recognize the crucial moments required to master their own changes, and it cost them dearly. Alexander the Great didn't recognize it, and neither did Napoleon. On the other hand, George Washington was an expert at mastering change. So were Gandhi and Martin Luther King, Jr."

"I'd love to do that Coach, I really would, but I just don't know how to get past the betrayal and the feelings from all of that," said Christopher sheepishly. "It's hard for me to trust people anymore, and I've turned back to alcohol just to sleep. I keep on thinking about our employees. They were dropped out there without a safety net—and I feel like it's all on my shoulders."

Christopher's despair sounded very similar to how Coach felt when he'd realized that he had not been able to help Danny. Chase, Sparks, and Shannon had reminded him that love, choosing what truly defines you, and contagious enthusiasm could truly change one's life; they were lessons that needed to be shared with the man sitting in front of him.

"Christopher," Coach began, "you have to realize that you're in a hole, and the only thing that can bring you out of that hole is you. This is your moment to master change. You have to decide if you want to move forward or wallow in self-pity. From what I know about you, you have a brilliant mind with a genuine desire to change the world. That is your direction. Your initiatives to change finance in this country helped more people than you can ever imagine. You don't have to lose that desire just because you are changing careers. You said it yourself that you value being a part of something that will help the less fortunate. That is your indicator of where your heart lies. Do not lose focus of your passion."

Christopher was bobbing his head in agreement and a smile returned to his face. "You know, Coach, I don't think it's very smart at 51 to change careers. But I'd like to do something totally different. Helping others, even if I never got to meet them, gave me a deep sense of satisfaction."

"Do you have any prospective moves so far?" asked Coach.

"A few…well, more than a few, actually, but I just want to choose something that fits for me," Christopher said. "It has to be something pure and meaningful to others. I've been strongly drawn to charity work. Last year, I visited the Make-A-Wish Foundation chapter here in St. Louis, and I felt like a kid in a candy store. In all of this drama with my company, it's consistently been on my mind."

"You sure you won't miss the three-piece suits and private jets?" Coach joked.

Christopher sighed. "I would be lying if I didn't say that that is one of the biggest things standing in my way—maybe the biggest. You get used to a certain kind of salary, a certain lifestyle—and you forget that you used to survive on a fraction of that. But you're so correct on the topic of values. Coming here and meeting with you has made me consider what truly appeals to me—the stuff you can't quantify or place a value on. You've renewed my trust by your patience and kindness in just meeting with me. I knew that I would get a great word of leadership from you, like so many young men before me. In truth, I value security and trust and I want to give that to other people. I tried to do that with Acres Financial Group but that time has passed…I just have to accept that. Now, as you say, I have to master my own change and pursue my passion."

"You'll get there, Christopher. Please stay in touch with me," said Coach, getting to his feet. They both shook hands as Coach made his way towards the door. He turned one last time and saw Christopher staring into the street, his gaze full of life and a smile stretching across his face. Coach had seen him enter the diner questioning the destruction of his past but after just a few minutes of candid conversation, he was convinced that Christopher was now pondering the great hope he'd give to others in his future.

CHAPTER 6

Michelle

Coach strode down the street from Vic's, enjoying the nice Sunday afternoon breeze. The sun was shining radiantly against the parked cars, and seemed to give life to everything in its path. The birds chirped their song to one another and Coach could hear children playing across the street in Citygarden—a popular, art park in the heart of downtown St. Louis. With no set plans for the next hour, he decided to take the long route back to his car by taking a stroll and taking in some sights.

After he crossed the street, he saw the granite statue of a man leaning against a cut marble fountain, which cascaded through the carefully manicured grass at the edge of the park. Coach walked deeper inside and admired the beauty and splendor of the birch and cypress trees that lined the walkway. A family of bicyclists sped past Coach, with two little girls bringing up the rear. He smiled and began to review his conversation with Christopher on values. Though he was sure that he'd been able to help him understand that he needed to master his own change in his life, the discussion prompted Coach to examine what he truly valued in himself. The past seventy-two hours had shown him that discussing life with others exhilarated him just as much as coaching basketball or connecting with students while giving history lectures. He felt as though his outlook was being reshaped into something more powerful and alive than before.

As Coach turned to the right, he was offered a remarkable view. A row of trees, flowers, and emerald shrubbery branched alongside the concrete walkway as it stretched through the park. In the foreground, Coach could see people lounging in the grass or moving to and fro. The sunlight gleamed off of the skyscrapers in the background and, beyond it all, as though it were a suspended guardian in the heavens, was the magnificent Gateway Arch of St. Louis.

Directly in front of Coach was a twelve-foot tall, brilliant red construction of a screw—or was that a light-bulb without the glass?—positioned on top of a circular platform, and supported by what appeared to be letters. A few people were gathered around the sculpture, one of many scattered throughout the park, and as Coach watched them from afar, he spotted a young woman to the right of the construction who was also watching. She was sitting on the concrete and her wild hair was flowing freely in the warm breeze. Even from a distance, Coach could tell that her shapeless, long-sleeved t-shirt and oversized pants looked as though they would have fit a man better than her, and her disheveled appearance gave him the impression that she was homeless. Next to her was a black garbage bag and a sign with scratchy handwriting that read: "Anything helps."

Coach felt sad as he looked at the young woman: sad for whatever circumstances had taken her to that point, sad that she hadn't gotten herself out, sad that she had probably once had dreams for herself that looked a lot different than this. But, truth be told, he was also feeling a little self-satisfied, too. He'd just had a handful of wonderful interactions with students who had enjoyed personal and professional success—and who mentioned that they had looked up to him in one way or another as a mentor.

He couldn't help but feel that it reflected well on him that he had managed to reach so many young people. He felt sorry that this woman may have been lacking such guidance in her own schooling experience.

But he couldn't seem to shake that young woman from his peripheral vision or his peripheral thoughts, so after a few minutes of debating with himself, Coach marched through the small crowd of onlookers and walked towards the scruffy figure, who looked to him to be in her early thirties. She took her eyes off of the statue and turned towards him with a sad smile.

"Interesting piece, right?" he said in a friendly tone, gesturing his thumb towards the artwork.

"I keep on wondering how these artists measure worth," she responded. "All around this park you'll find some of the most unique structures and pieces, none of them the same, but all of them valuable in some way. However, to the untrained eye, they could be ugly or weird or strange."

"There's that old saying that beauty is in the eye of the beholder," he said.

She nodded. "I agree. We assign value selectively to works of art. I could read a book that I love and you could think it was horrible. I think we treat people the same way."

Coach paused for a moment. He could feel the crisp twenty dollar bill in his pocket, which he'd initially planned to give to the young woman. But he wanted to talk with her more, like he had with Christopher and Shannon, to see if he could give her more than a few bucks—or learn something from her.

"Is this seat taken?" Coach asked, gesturing to the pavement next to her. The woman chuckled and said, "No."

Coach gingerly eased himself down, now intrigued. "That's an interesting analysis Miss…?" said Coach.

"Michelle," she said for him. "And I know you, Coach Coleman, but you probably don't remember me that much. I skipped school a lot back when I went to Thompson High, but I always loved your classes. I'd have a joint or two at my lunch break—if I decided to come to school at all—but I loved to listen to you craft your lessons with such beauty. They were the highlight of my days."

Every ounce of smugness he had been feeling at his own abilities as a mentor drained away. Coach forced a smile. "Pleasure to meet you…again, I guess, Michelle—and I'm glad you were able to get the essence of my class. Although I'm sorry you didn't stop by more often."

"I'm sorry too," she replied, staring off into the distance.

Coach had seen a small sandwich shop within the park, and he suddenly had a bright idea.

"Would you like for me to grab you some lunch?" he asked Michelle.

———

Ten minutes later, when Michelle was halfway through her roast beef sandwich, Coach gazed at their new surroundings. They were sitting on a bench overlooking a clearing in the park. To their left was a massive statue of a head laid to its side, positioned in the center of an onyx tiled, circular formation. It had taken him a few minutes to remember Michelle clearly. He soon recalled that she'd always been tardy to his class. She had been a sharp student with a bright, open mind, but he'd always hoped that she would have applied it a little better than she had.

"I used to love your essays. History is usually written with a very factual, to-the-point analysis, but you would drift back and forth into philosophy. I liked that so much that I used to give you extra credit just for your ideas," said Coach. "But you must have left Thompson because as I recall, I stopped seeing you during your senior year altogether."

"That's true," she answered regretfully. "School just felt too slow for me in those days, so I decided to get my GED and go straight to community college. I did all right for a while—I actually started attending my classes, I mean. I ended up taking about every major you could think of, but nothing ever seemed to fit. To be honest, that's the story of my life. I've always imagined that I was that missing puzzle piece that never could quite connect into the rest of the society. I remember writing a letter to myself once titled 'Do We Live by Default or Design'?"

Coach thought over her comment. "What were your conclusions?"

"As a jaded optimist, I'd say I'm fundamentally designed to look forever for something better that I don't have or that I need. So, by default, I'm screwed in every sense of the word," she said with a heavy laugh.

"Well, you still rationalize like a philosopher," Coach said. "But what makes you say that about yourself? Surely you haven't lived your entire life yet, so the best could be ahead of you."

"That's the problem Coach, I don't know how to have a filter for what could be good or bad for me. I just get anxious for sudden change, and I'm unable to wait for good things to develop. I've never been able to live a day-to-day existence without becoming completely bored. That's why I couldn't cut it at Thompson and why I flunked out of community college. After that, I worked a bunch of waitressing jobs and then at a leasing center for an apartment complex. They were respectable jobs with good people, but I never could kick that drug habit and got fired time after time. When money got low, I lived out of my car, and then sold that for some more money, and lived with a bunch of different guys that I dated. Each time things would start to get settled, I'd get so anxious that my heart would race. I wanted more for myself but didn't have the patience to develop it."

"You didn't have a stake anywhere," Coach said, shaking his head slowly.

"Nope, not at all. On a whim, I decided to move to Florida—Cocoa Beach, to be exact. I'd gone there as a child and I remember it being so beautiful. It was the first and last time I'd ever been to a beach, which was so open and free that it reminded me of myself."

Michelle's expressions were wide and energetic as she spoke about this time of her life. Coach could tell that she was a true extrovert who lived entirely by her senses and impulses and seemed to be recharging even as she interacted with him.

"I wanted a fresh start so I bought a bus ticket, and didn't look back. I worked for a few years doing odd jobs, made a little bit of money, and even managed to get clean with the help of some programs at a local church. Then I met Barry, a real estate agent who sold property along the Florida coastline." Michelle paused and sighed. Her energy faded. "We had a great relationship and the thought of settling down crossed my mind. We were engaged, living in a nice home, and for the first time, I thought that I could actually be happy. But Barry wasn't satisfied with that. Let's just say that he didn't believe in monogamy and when he was on the road, he had too many other friends keeping him busy. When I'd had enough of his lies, I left our home and didn't tell him where I was going. That was a year ago. I've been back here in St. Louis—home sweet home—ever since."

Coach took a deep sigh. "You've been through a lot, Michelle. I am sorry to see your situation hasn't improved presently. Where are your parents?"

"They divorced a few years ago, when I was gone. I had no contact with them so I didn't know," she said hurriedly. "Now my mother lives in L.A. with Fred, a mid-level producer, and my dad lives in Dallas with his new wife. I got back in touch with both of them recently, but I get the feeling that they'd rather keep their distance. I haven't seen them yet because I don't want to see the pain in their faces. Since I disappeared without a trace all those years ago, I know that hurt them a lot. So I haven't intruded on them anymore. I've just been on the streets and living in shelters holding on to the hope that something positive will happen for me sooner or later here, but I don't know…"

Coach thought about the confusion and frustration that had kept him from contacting Chase for three years, and he suddenly felt guilty. Even though he'd now reconciled with his son, it did not feel good hearing Michelle talk about her own isolation from her parents.

She could see the look on his face. "See? I told you I was designed to default! Don't cry on me, Coach. You asked to hear my story."

He smiled. "It's not that, I'm just wondering what kind of action you'll take now. You've said that you hope something positive will happen for you—but why wait for it? I just spoke with a friend this morning on mastering the changes in our lives. Here you are, with a blank slate, and you can make yourself into whatever you desire to be. You just have to choose what direction works for you."

"I've never chosen wisely," exclaimed Michelle, tugging back a strand of hair behind her ear.

"Then don't choose by impulse—or default, as you say. Choose with strategy, planning, and with a goal in mind. You've lived your life by your emotions and what feels good at the time, but have you ever given any thought to designing your own happiness?"

Michelle shook her head, so Coach continued speaking.

"No matter where you live, who you date, or how much money you have or don't have, only you can find peace with yourself. Only you can design your own happy future. As a philosopher, I'd imagine you'd understand this concept very well," he said.

"Those words sound good, Coach, and I have to be honest with you. I've never been a planner of any sorts," said Michelle. "Somehow, committing to anything—even to a plan—felt like settling."

"That's fine. But if you fail to plan, then you're only planning to fail. That's what I always tell my players at Thompson High. The grass isn't always greener on the other side."

Michelle laughed. "It only looks greener because of what it's been fertilized with—and you know that's some nasty stuff."

Coach grinned. In front of him, a child was busy kicking a soccer ball as his mom watched. Coach turned to Michelle. "You have to design the life you want," he repeated, "and the first thing to do is to find employment."

"You mean I can't always be a whimsical bum ranting about philosophy?" she replied sarcastically.

"I'm not sure the salary is very high for a position like that," Coach joked. "But really, what do you really want?"

Michelle stiffened and clenched her jaw. "Purpose. Discipline. The fortitude to push forward and get results on my own terms.

Well," she paused. "That's not what I want...but it's probably what I need."

Coach stood to his feet. "Michelle, I'd like to help you create your design. If you don't mind, I'd like to give you a ride to the outlet mall and buy you a set of professional work clothes. After that, I can take you back to your shelter. Tomorrow morning we can both go to a temp agency to meet a friend of mine who I think could help you with the next steps of planning your future. Does that sound good?"

Michelle thought for a moment before smiling in agreement. "I want to live well and consistently, Coach. For so long I've thought that I was flawed and was too afraid to make any steps because they usually end in failure. Talking with you today has shown me that maybe I can create my own design for once."

"So you'll come with me?" asked Coach, hopefully.

"Of course," Michelle said, now standing as well. She pointed towards the statue of the head. "You know, these artists had to have a vision of their pieces at some point, long before it had been developed. I'd like to do the same with my own life."

"That's the spirit, Michelle! One day, you'll be able to see the finished product. But you just have to start first," Coach promised.

CHAPTER 7

Gloria

The next afternoon, a warm Monday, Coach was waiting for Michelle outside a local emergency shelter that provided temporary housing to at-risk women. They had spent a wonderful Sunday afternoon together shopping for work and casual clothing for Michelle. After they finished, Coach took her to a library where he helped her write up and print out her resume. As their day had worn on, their talks moved from one subject to the next—from Coach's reconciliation with Chase, to Michelle's fascination with spray tans, snow birds, and other whimsical observations she'd picked up in Florida. They'd had an entertaining time, and Coach was surprised at just how much he'd learned from Michelle in their exchanges.

Which was why it concerned him so much that she was ten minutes late for him to pick her up. For the third time, Coach peered down at his watch and wondered where she was. Then, the door to the shelter opened and Michelle bounded out. She was wearing her brand new work clothes and had straightened her hair. Coach leaned over and opened the passenger door.

"You look like a million bucks!" he said. "Good morning! The next phase of your life begins today."

Michelle smiled but didn't make eye contact with him. She climbed inside the SUV, shut the door, and gave a huge sigh. "Coach, I almost didn't come out today."

"Why not?" he asked.

"I just don't want to be a burden on you. I mean, you should be in your classroom and not helping out some bum."

He waved her away dismissively. "Please, don't think that. This is the final week of classes, and I only have meetings after school—all of which I can move around. I assure you that you are not intruding. And you're not a bum, you're my friend. My friends are all rock stars, not bums."

Michelle smiled. She'd regained some comfort from his words. "Thanks Coach. I needed that."

They set off for the temp agency. Coach advised Michelle that she should be patient with herself whenever she developed any goal. Success was not going to happen overnight, and he wanted her to really take that point to heart. "Maximize every moment and enjoy all of the small things that make up your day. Keep your notebook to jot down some of your ideas, and make a practical, strict schedule. I think it will also help you to have a very assertive accountability partner who'll help you stay on track with your game plan."

Before long, they arrived at the temp agency. Coach parked his car out front and turned to Michelle. "Ready to go?" he asked.

She clenched her jaw and her hands were squeezing against her notebook. "I'm not sure if I can do this Coach. I don't even know what to say. What if they ask me what I've been doing for the past eight years of my life? What do I say?"

"Michelle, relax," Coach said soothingly. "I'll coach you through this."

They began to run through a practiced set of introductions and professional work history for Michelle to share during her meeting. Her mind was like a sponge; she remembered the pitch on her second try. She even took notes. As she grew more and more confident, Coach could see that she would do well when she had enough structure.

They entered the temp agency together, "We have an appointment with Gloria," Coach told the receptionist.

"Right this way," she replied.

Michelle flashed Coach a smile of strength and headed back into the room. Coach remained in the waiting room and casually watched as people came and went. Some of them had blank expressions on their faces, and others would emerge from the back offices with a look of joy. One thing that everyone had in common was that they looked as though life had been weighing them down, and all they needed was a helping hand to get back in shape. Coach was suddenly grateful for the illustrious career, stability, and chances that he'd been able to have at Thompson High. No one was safe from the sudden surprises of life.

You could live like Christopher and before you know it, a life-altering experience could send you on a downward spiral. Overnight, anyone could become like Michelle, thought Coach. A young man exited from the back with a huge grin on his face. *Or, you could be like Sparks and Shannon, and determine what creates your own passion and direction in life. Ultimately, it all comes down to how you choose to respond to circumstances.*

"Coach Coleman?" said the receptionist, searching the waiting room crowd.

He stood to his feet. "Yes?"

"Gloria would like to see you for a moment."

Coach brushed himself off and followed the receptionist to the office where Michelle was sitting. The human resources director Gloria Enriquez—also a former pupil and friend of

Coach—was sitting before her and stood when he entered.

"Gloria, great to see you again!" Coach said, shaking her hand.

"Coach Coleman, I am so happy to see you as well," she replied warmly. "Michelle was just telling me about how you inspired her to come here. When I heard you were with her, I just had to say hello to you. Michelle—" Gloria turned towards her "—could you excuse us for just one moment?"

Michelle nodded. She had an air of confidence and pride as she left the office, which pleased Coach. *The interview must have gone well*, he thought with joy.

As Michelle closed the door, Coach turned to Gloria and said, "She's a real trooper, isn't she?"

Gloria pulled her hair into a tight ponytail and, when she spoke, her tone was flat and serious. "That's what I wanted to talk to you about, Coach. Since Michelle put you as her emergency contact, I thought it would be best to speak with you about a few concerns I have with her resume. I read through the copy you emailed me before our interview this morning, and her sporadic movement raises a few red flags with me."

"Understandable," Coach said. "Are there any problems?"

Gloria's black pupils darted towards Michelle's file. "Michelle is a wonderful person. We sat here for twenty minutes just talking about life. She's truly remarkable…and I won't get into specifics, but my concerns were about her ability to remain stable," she admitted. "Her resume is all over the place and I'm afraid that she'll only job jump. I'm fine with whatever my clients decide to do with their lives, but there are people out there who need employment and I don't want her to treat this as a game."

"I was talking to Michelle about getting an accountability partner to help her remain sober and focused on her goals,"

Coach explained. "I'm not asking for any special favors that might put your job or your relationship with your clients in jeopardy, but I just wanted to help Michelle believe in herself enough to stick something out. Each small goal leads to a larger one."

Gloria peered nervously at a photo to the right of her desk, where she was pictured with her husband.

Coach raised an eyebrow and sensed an opportunity to connect with Gloria, his old friend and former pupil.

"By the way Gloria, you look amazing. Last time we talked over lunch, about two years ago I recall, you were going through some tough circumstances."

Her nostrils flared at the memory. "Coach, those have considerably improved, but I'm still dealing with some emotional issues," said Gloria. "My husband and I had an argument this past week, and he started to raise his voice but then caught himself and remained calm. The thought of going through those anger issues with him again just broke me down. When I saw you a couple of years ago, we'd just had a particularly awful fight and I didn't know what to do. Since then, Sam and I have been to marriage counseling for our issues and he's even sought anger management separately. He's improved Coach. We've improved. Still, it scared me. I still judge him the way I did a few years ago, and that bothers me. I'm just not sure if I have the emotional reserves to take on another commitment like Michelle."

"I'm sorry that experience has triggered fear in you. But please don't let it derail your focus. Remember what we talked about a few years ago? You had a goal of taking Sam to counseling and applying yourself more aggressively at work. Now you're the human resources director and, as you mentioned in your email last month, counseling is going great for the both of you," Coach said.

"Thanks, Coach. And it has. It's just that I am still struggling emotionally. I grew up in a, well, a very *opinionated* family so I'm always worried at how I'll be defined if they all knew about the problems I've been through, or that they will label me as 'stupid' or 'in denial' because I didn't leave Sam. Because of that, I tend to prejudge things a lot more than usual these days, especially after I took this position," Gloria replied. She gestured to a stack of files on her desk. "I make my living judging others to see if they are suitable for a position through us. I have to keep the needs and trust of the employer in mind, and also see if the applicant can perform the work required. It's a filtering process, but I usually know in my mind whether or not the person will pass my initial inspection before they even walk through the door."

"Have you always been right?" asked Coach.

"If I pass an applicant along to an employer, then I have to have full faith that I made the right decision. If I do not pass them on, then I'll never know. I am too focused on the next file to stress myself out with that," Gloria said.

"You've always had nerves of steel, Gloria," Coach commented.

"You have to, working here!" she exclaimed.

"But the truth is, you've been wrong before, and so have I, and every other person in this world," Coach reasoned. "In your emails with me, you've said that you and Sam have a wonderful marriage now. If any passerby would have prejudged that two years ago, then they wouldn't have faith in its success."

"The truth is Coach, I'd like to be more open-minded in that regard. I don't want to judge people so much that it becomes second nature. That's not the person I am," Gloria answered. "I feel like I've become jaded."

"I find it ironic that you are **worried** about how you are defined by others, but you spend all day reviewing files and doing the same to people. You judge them based on sheets of paper rather than real interactions. That's probably why it's bothering you," he said with intrigue.

"Exactly, Coach. And it affects the way I interview them," she confessed. "But what's more, I feel as though I take this scrutiny everywhere else in my life. Like Sam, or my boss for that matter. I have an impression or opinion of them and it's very tough to break, even if they have shown evidence of real and lasting change. I don't want to think Sam is a threat to me, and I don't like seeing my boss in a negative light. Sure, she's a bit over-bearing at times— but only because she knows my potential and wants to push me to perform at my highest level. She's not a mean person, but I find myself thinking that in our interactions. How do I stop this?"

"But isn't that just human nature?" Coach asked, crossing his legs. "We're always judgmental of others, whether we are reading about them in the paper, watching them walk down the street, or in even our private moments with friends. We immediately assume things about them."

Coach briefly shared with her his past few days and how he had gone into every interaction expecting something different than what had come of it. "With Michelle, I wanted to serve more and help her design her own path in life. If I would have refused to look past my prejudgments of any of these people, I'd have missed the opportunity to gain important insight and life lessons," Coach said. "We have to try and defy the human nature that comes with judging others. This allows us to be more open to the people to whom we are willing to give a chance."

"That is very wise, Coach," said Gloria with a smile.

"So…" he began, hoping she would chime in.

"So?"

"So, in order to get out of this rut, maybe you can do a more extensive method of measuring people," he urged. "Try to find things in your interview that aren't on the page. I think that every piece of information is valuable in this sense, because you are always going to be making worthiness calls on your clients—and people in your life, in general. That's simply the nature of things. But if you work to defy that natural instinct that we all have to make decisions based only on surface impressions, you can find so much more. I mean, within reason, of course. Sometimes there are going to be people or situations that are completely negative and you have to sever that connection to protect yourself. But in everyday life, you can find much more joy if you are determined to operate from a place of grace and understanding."

Gloria was starting to smile. "So what you're saying is that living in fear or unhappiness is taking the easy way out, even though it's harder in the end. There's a lot of bad stuff in this world—but anyone can see that. It doesn't take any effort to be cynical and jaded about that, but it does take a little more courage to look past and find the potential for good."

"You just said it better than I could have," Coach answered.

"I need to do this," Gloria nodded slowly. "Effective: today."

Gloria dialed the receptionist and asked her to bring Michelle back to the office. Michelle entered the room and rejoined them. She was still smiling and encouraged.

"Michelle, Coach mentioned to me that you'd be interested in an accountability partner," Gloria said. "I'd love to help you out with this as you proceed forward with us."

Michelle gasped, then tried to regain her composure. "Yes! I'm very happy to hear that, and I would love to."

Gloria returned her smile, and stared down at her paperwork. She tapped her pen against her desk and bit her lip. "You know... I'd like you to do something for me, Michelle, as we try to match you to the best position. This question isn't something I usually ask but I was wondering if you could write out a short response to a question. There is no right or wrong response—it's just something I'd like you to be aware of so that I can understand you better and can tailor our interactions to your goals: '*How do you measure your worth?*'"

When Gloria finished the question, Coach noticed a few things happening. He saw her facial expression consider the question personally, as if she were asking herself the same thing. As Michelle wrote on her sheet of paper in silence, Coach could see Gloria evaluating the weight of their conversation in her mind, and in Gloria's genuine smile and peaceful demeanor, he saw a person changed.

CHAPTER 8

The Commencement Speech

That Friday, the bleachers of the brand new Thompson High gymnasium—completed only three weeks earlier—were now packed with families, friends, professional staff, and teachers waiting to celebrate with the graduates. A cacophony of conversations filled the expansive, brightly-painted yellow and blue gym as they waited for the event to begin. Seated on the floor of the gym were the graduates, all smiling and waving to acquaintances in the crowd. Many of them had their mobile phones out and were taking selfies or recording video. Pomp and circumstance played from the speakers, and a buzz of excitement hung in the air. Coach was taking it all in just out of view past the bleachers. His commencement speech would be underway in only a few minutes, and he would take the stage for one final message to the school that had been so good to him for more than thirty-three years.

The crowd hushed as Dr. Gibbs, principal of Thompson High, stepped to the podium and began her opening remarks. As she spoke, Coach felt the energy pulse through the gymnasium. The students were sitting with nervous excitement, happy about the great adventure they were able to complete and ready for the even greater ones that lay ahead.

And so was he. It had been one week since Danny's funeral, and Coach had never imagined that moment would send him on an unexpected adventure of perspective, discovery, and purpose. Now here he was, standing for the last time in a place that he treasured, with a message on his heart. In his hands, Coach held the commencement speech he had furiously edited only hours before Danny's mother had given him that fateful phone call last week.

"...with that being said, I'd like to invite up a very special member of the Thompson High School family. He's a five-time Teacher of the Year award winner, five time state championship-winning coach, and a remarkable friend to all. Please welcome your very own Coach Coleman to the stage!" Dr. Gibbs said, gesturing towards him.

Coach stepped forward to thunderous applause. He clenched his rolled up speech in hand as he waved to the crowd. As he approached the podium, the students and audience rose to their feet. The principal and superintendent shook his hand.

"Coach, before you begin, I'd like to personally thank you for your thirty-three years of service," said the principal. "So many people have had the opportunity to have been taught, coached, and prepared for life, by you. There are no sufficient words or deeds to encompass all you have done for our community, but on behalf of the entire Thompson High School family, I'd like to thank you for your decades of dedication to our school. Here is a small token of our appreciation." She paused and gestured with her hand to the ceiling. Everyone peered up and followed her direction. There was a row of covered drapes hanging from the rafters, next to the five Thompson High basketball state championship banners.

"Three...two...one!" shouted the principal.

The drapes dropped—revealing a yellow and blue colored banner, with the lettering spelling out "Coach Michael Coleman Gymnasium." Positioned next to it was an honorary Knights jersey with his name on the back. The entire gymnasium thundered in applause. Coach felt his mouth fall open and tears come to his eyes as the cheers bounced off the walls.

"Who better to name our gym after than the most legendary coach in Thompson High School history?" Dr. Gibbs said, leaning into the microphone. "Coach, we just wanted to say thank you in the most honest way possible. Though we are saddened that you are leaving us, you will never be forgotten here. And now, without further ado, you may address our graduating seniors."

Another roar of applause lit up the gymnasium. Coach waved to the sea of faces before him, all of who seemed to have had a story or a moment shared with him. When the applause finally died down, Coach stared at his typed speech as it lay curling on the podium. He gazed forward into the audience. There, sitting on the front row, was Chase, smiling proudly and flashing him a thumbs up.

Coach nervously peered out at the students, and down to his speech, and then repeated the action. He could feel the adrenaline pumping through his entire body as every eye in the packed gym—*his* gym—was fixed on him, waiting for him to begin to speak. One week ago, he'd been standing before a family who'd lost one of their own and had struggled to get out more than few words. Today, he was celebrating a successful career and his commitment to Thompson High, with more than three thousand people in attendance. How many of these faces would he still remember in five years? In ten? How many Dannys were sitting before him right now—maybe not the most gifted student or remarkable athlete, but important and deserving in their own way, desperately seeking a sense of significance? All week, he'd experienced one profound moment after another of human connection, where he'd been able to see, reflect on, and understand his true purpose.

And then, as though he'd been struck by lightning, Coach realized that this speech was an opportunity to help many others find their own.

He folded his prepared words in half and placed them in his pocket.

"You know, I've been working all month on my speech, preparing for tonight," he began candidly. "I've taught at this school for thirty-three years, and I've always wondered what I would say if I were ever asked to speak at a graduation. But I just realized that I don't want to read you a series of clichés or tired words that you probably won't be able to recall in a year. I just want to say a few words from the heart right now, in this moment."

Coach surveyed everyone in attendance, and he realized that he'd captured their full attention.

"Last Friday, I spoke at a funeral of one of my former students who took his own life."

The audience went completely silent. Coach paused as a general expression of shock spread across the faces of all attendees.

"At that funeral I quoted Mark Twain and told the grieving

family that 'The two most important days of your life are the day you are born, and the day you discover why.' I desperately wish I could have shown that young man how to discover his 'why' when I had the chance, and that I could have told everyone at the funeral how to find their own purpose for themselves.

"But in that moment, I didn't know what to say. In the classroom and on the basketball court over the last thirty-plus years I have never been at a loss for words or felt stumped—but last week I was. When it came to teaching the lesson that matters most in life, I felt that I let my former student down, along with his family and friends who were grieving his loss," Coach said, with a tear running down his cheek.

"I left that funeral with some heavy thoughts. Little did I know that I was about to have the most amazing week of my life, which would put everything into perspective for me. And today, I want to give the speech that I wish I'd have given last week, to the family at that funeral.

"Everyone calls me 'Coach' but we are all coaches in some way," Coach paused, taking a moment to glance at the students themselves. "Students: You all are graduating high school and are going to go off and conquer the world. I'd expect nothing less from Thompson High graduates. I want you to be successful and do great things and be great achievers. More than that, though, I want you to be great people. Many of you may be asking yourselves 'What next?' You've gone through school and you're trying to find the people, places, and things that have the right answers. But the learning process isn't about finding the right answers, it is about asking the right questions. I'd like for all of you to realize that finding your purpose can begin right now, as you are sitting here. You don't have to wait until you are my age, or at a crossroads, wondering what direction you'll go next. All you have to do is ask yourselves the right questions and listen honestly as your soul whispers the answers.

"So what are those questions? The first thing is, *who are you serving?*" Coach said. He let the question hang for a moment. "We are all connected and one of the greatest lessons of life is to realize that your contribution makes you great. The moment you walk out of this gymnasium, go find someone else to serve. Maybe you could start with hugging your mom or dad, your grandparents, and your support group—and thanking them for bringing you this far. But then, keep going. Find someone who you can coach and help get through their own difficult times. You'll never know how much impact you'll have on a person's life by just listening to them. I promise you will also find yourself when you freely give to others. Like Florence Nightingale, the great social reformer and humanitarian, we should all give more and take less.

We are all infinitely blessed in many ways, and we owe it to society to give something back. My son Chase reminded me this week of this important truth: Service improves the lives of others but its greatest reward is the enrichment and new meaning that it will bring your own life." Coach motioned towards Chase, who was smiling from his seat. "Thank you son, for this wonderful reminder."

Chase smiled at his dad proudly. His eyes were wet with tears.

"Next, ask yourself, *what are your defining moments?* It's very easy to remember the bad situations and problems of our lives. The truth of life is that we will all fail at something or face setbacks, but it's how we respond to those obstacles that speak volumes about our character. It is in our toughest trials and through our critical choices that we determine who we are. When life gets hard—and trust me, it will—don't lose faith in the end of your story. Life will send many unexpected challenges your way, but you must master those changes with grace. I would have never been able to win those state championships for Thompson High if I did not have a capable group of young men and staff who knew how to respond to sudden changes. As you move forward in life, I implore you to learn how to adapt, regroup, and push on. George Washington, Susan B. Anthony, and Mahatma Gandhi were all masters of change. They did not allow the challenges of life to beat them into complacency. This is a profound lesson that I'd like to emphasize to you. *When a defining moment comes along, you define the moment…or the moment defines you.*

"Thirdly, *what is your passion?* In your journey into the world, you'll discover what truly makes you come alive. For some of you, it could be academics, sports, or creativity. For others, it could be humanitarianism, volunteer work, or dedication to a cause. For example, in physics, the second law of thermodynamics is called entropy." Coach glanced over to where the teachers were sitting and said, "You didn't think I knew that, did you, Mrs. Snyder?"

Laughter erupted in the gym. Coach smiled and continued, "The law states that nature tends toward chaos, and the truth of that law is that people and things are drawn to energy. Passion creates emotion—or energy in motion. When you have passion, that energy will move you and people will follow. It will light you with a fire that is impossible to ignore. Many of you may not be aware of it, but your passion may be right in front of you and waiting for you to engage it, to feed it with life and fire. You have all heard me quote many great figures in history, but the most poignant quote I have ever found may be by Martin Luther King, Jr., when he said, 'If you haven't discovered something worth dying for, you haven't found anything worth living for.' Think about those words for a moment. Search inside yourself to find what truly ignites you.

"This journey of self-discovery will only grow deeper as you move forward. In your passion you'll find your own definition of success. So you must then ask yourself, *what do you value?* And *how do you measure your own worth?* Graduates, don't be fooled. Money, material gains, and powerful people will not be the key to your happiness. You must have a healthy vision of who you are and how you see yourself. If you are not happy, superficiality will not solve that problem.

"I've talked to people this week who have had it all and some who have nothing, and they were all seeking the same thing: purpose. Each of us has to find our place in this world, our calling and our contribution. The world is a big place, but it always has enough space for us to make a meaningful impact. When you honestly reflect on your life, you will realize just how important your purpose is.

"As you leave Thompson High and go forth into the world, I want to challenge you to learn these lessons *now*. Take authority over your own lives with these questions. We want you to go and achieve and do great things and be successful, but more importantly, my goal as a coach and a teacher was always to help you be great people."

Coach paused as the tears began to flow. But he felt motivated, as though he'd just won another state championship. The nervousness that had initially gnawed at him had now been replaced by a strong sense of empowerment. The students and their parents were hanging on to his every word, and Coach could feel the love in the room.

"And as you become a great person, you will find that you are helping others to be better, as well. We are all coaches. We are all motivators and encouragers. We have one thing in common: We were all born. We've all had that first day. And let's be honest—you didn't have a whole lot to do with that. It's not really something you can take credit for," he said with a smile as he peered into the eyes of as many students as he could. "We've been fortunate enough to have had that first day, and we are all seeking the answers to find that second day. So as you leave the ceremony, I want you to focus on the right questions:

Who are you serving?

What are your defining moments?

What is your passion?

What do you value?

How do you measure your own worth?

"You won't be disappointed with the results and, in time, you'll find your purpose. You'll understand why that first day happened—and what you're supposed to do about it. I can think of no greater wish for each of you at this moment of graduation than this:

"May you discover your second day."

ABOUT
THE
AUTHORS

Author Chad Hymas

The Wall Street Journal calls Chad Hymas "one of the 10 most inspirational people in the World!"

Chad inspires, motivates, and moves audiences, creating an experience that touches hearts for a lifetime. He is one of the youngest ever to receive the Council of Peers Award for Excellence (CPAE) and to be inducted into the prestigious National Speaker Hall Of Fame.

In 2001, at the age of 27, Chad's life changed in an instant when a 2,000-pound bale of hay shattered his neck leaving him a quadriplegic. But Chad's dreams were not paralyzed that day—he became an example of what is possible.

Chad is a best-selling author, president of his own Communications Company, Chad Hymas Communications, Inc., and is a recognized world-class wheelchair athlete. In 2003, Chad set a world record by wheeling his chair from Salt Lake City to Las Vegas (513 miles).

Chad's speaking career in the areas of leadership, team building, customer service, and mastering change has brought him multiple honors. He is the past president of the National Speakers Association Utah chapter and a member of the exclusive elite Speakers Roundtable (one of twenty of the world's top speakers).

As a member of the National Speakers Association, Chad travels as many as 300,000 miles a year captivating and entertaining audiences around the world. He has graced the stage of hundreds of professional and civic organizations including Wells Fargo, Blue Cross Blue Shield, AT&T, Rainbird, IHC, American Express, Prudential Life, Vast FX, and Merrill Lynch.

Author Ty Bennett

When Ty was 21 years old, he and his brother Scott started a business in direct sales, which they built to over $20 million in annual revenue while still in their twenties. Since that time, he has developed over 500 sales managers globally with sales and leadership in 37 countries. As a young entrepreneur, Ty continues to engage his team's focus to grow sales. He uses the power of influence and storytelling to get buy-in to the vision of growing their multimillion-dollar sales organization.

With a natural ability to engage and empower others, Ty draws on his experience in the trenches to share real and tangible techniques about the principles of leadership that continue to create his success. The founder of Leadership Inc. who has been featured as one of the *Top 40 Under 40*, Ty is a young fresh voice providing interactive presentations that are engaging, dynamic and inspiring.

His clients include some of the most recognizable brands in the world such as: Coca-Cola, Subway, Wounded Warrior Project, Blue Cross Blue Shield and Remax. Ty has shared the stage with celebrities, Olympians and world-renowned thought leaders such as *President Bush and President Clinton.*

Ty's best-selling books—*The Power of Influence and The Power of Storytelling: The Art of Influential Communication*—are used in graduate courses at multiple universities including MIT, as today's version of "How to Win Friends and Influence People."

Ty lives in Utah with his wife Sarah, daughters Andie and Lizzy and sons Tanner and Drew.

Author Don Yaeger

Don Yaeger is a nationally acclaimed inspirational speaker, longtime Associate Editor of *Sports Illustrated* and author of 24 books, eight of which have become New York Times Best-sellers. He began his career at the San Antonio (TX) Light and also worked at the Dallas Morning News and the Florida Times-Union in Jacksonville before going to work for *Sports Illustrated*.

As an author, Don has written books with, among others, Hall of Fame running back Walter Payton, UCLA basketball Coach John Wooden, baseball legends John Smoltz and Tug McGraw and football stars Warrick Dunn and Michael Oher (featured in the movie *The Blind Side*). He teamed with Fox News anchor Brian Kilmeade to pen the 2013 best-seller "*George Washington's Secret Six*," a look at the citizen spy ring that helped win the Revolutionary War.

Don left *Sports Illustrated* in 2008 to pursue a public speaking career that has allowed him to share stories learned from the greatest winners of our generation with audiences as diverse as Fortune 10 companies to cancer survivor groups, where he shares his personal story. More than a quarter-million people have heard his discussions on "What Makes the Great Ones Great." He has also built corporate programs on lessons from great sporting franchises on building Cultures of Success.

Learn more at www.donyaeger.com or contact Don at don@donyaeger.com